BURN

SINS Series Book 6

EMMA SLATE

Tabula Rasa Publishing

____

Chapter 1
QUINN

____

My name is Quinn O'Malley.

I was in a car accident.

I am engaged.

Three indisputable facts.

I repeated those sentences, chanting them like a mantra.

"Quinn?" a voice asked, dragging me from the black pit of my empty mind.

The man next to my bed had dark brown eyes and full lips. The man who'd just told me his name was Ori and that he was my fiancé.

Shouldn't my parents have been here? Their daughter had been in a car accident and—When I tried to picture my parents, nothing came to mind.

My breaths became sharp and shallow.

"Easy," the man said. "Remember to breathe."

Remember to breathe.

It was the only thing I could remember.

My name is Quinn O'Malley.

I was in a car accident.

I am engaged.

When I felt like I was under control, I asked, "Where are my parents?"

"They—you lost your parents."

"Both of them?"

The man—Ori—nodded.

A gaping hole of sadness opened up, and I started to cry. It was an instinctual reaction. I realized it even as I cried for the parents I didn't remember. I cried for the memories I'd lost. I cried because I didn't know what else to *do*.

Ori climbed into the hospital bed and held me to him. This man, my fiancé, a stranger. I took his comfort, clinging to him like a survivor in the middle of the ocean clung to driftwood.

He brushed the hair away from my face and whispered words of comfort, holding me and letting me soak the front of his gray shirt.

When the storm passed, I released my grip on him and tried to move away, suddenly embarrassed that I'd lost it in front of a man I didn't remember.

Ori let me go, but he didn't move away. He kept one hand on the back of my neck, his thumb rubbing slow, leisurely circles across my skin.

"I'm okay now," I assured him.

"I know."

"You can…stop touching me."

With a sigh, he dropped his hand.

"My parents are gone," I said.

"Yes."

"I don't have any family? Is that why you're the only one here?"

"I'm your family."

I stared at him, searching my memory, hoping for a

spark of recognition. He was handsome. Golden skin, dark hair, dark eyes, and full lips.

My gaze dropped to his mouth, which curved into a smile. I hastily looked away. Apparently, my lust suffered no amnesia.

I pinched the bridge of my nose. A headache was coming on. "I wish you could tell me everything."

"I'm not supposed to. The doctor said—well, you have extenuating circumstances."

"What does that mean?" I asked, releasing the column of my nose.

"It means you've had a rough go of it lately, and the doctor is concerned about…"

"Concerned about?" I pressed, hating that he'd stopped talking.

"Concerned that your mind isn't strong enough to handle it."

I blinked. "He thinks I'll crack."

Ori nodded slowly.

Great. So not only did I have amnesia, but I was deemed unstable.

A sudden burst of anger blasted through my veins. What right did they have to keep my memories from me?

I didn't even know what my own face looked like. Was I a blonde? Brunette? What color were my eyes? Desperate for answers, I slipped out of the hospital bed and trekked to the bathroom. My back was suddenly cold, and I looked behind me to see the hospital gown gaping open to reveal white lace panties.

Huh. Lace.

I glanced at Ori to find him staring at my backside. When he realized I'd caught him looking, he smiled and shrugged.

My eyes narrowed. I slipped into the bathroom and

flipped on the light—more florescent lighting—and peered into the mirror. Sleek, dark hair cut into a chin-length bob. Long fair neck. I stretched it and cocked my head to the side. Green eyes fringed with dark lashes. Green. That was interesting. I traced my high cheekbones and then my lips.

"You were a teen model," Ori said from the doorway.

I jumped, not having heard his approach. My glare met his gaze in the mirror.

"Sorry. Didn't mean to sneak up on you."

I nodded, accepting his apology. "A teen model? Really?"

He nodded. "Ralph Lauren."

"You're kidding."

Ori laughed. "No, I'm not kidding."

"Do you have pictures?"

"I—yeah. I have pictures."

"Are you going to show them to me?" I asked, crossing my arms over my chest.

For some reason, that made Ori's smile widen.

"What?" I demanded.

"Your attitude is coming back. I'm really happy about that."

I wasn't sure what to say, so I said nothing. I had attitude? I didn't *feel* like I had attitude. I felt like I was… empty. Blank. Waiting for others to draw on me so I had some color.

"You want to get out of here?" he asked.

I nodded. "Yeah. This place is so…depressing. Oh, I don't have clothes."

"I went to get a few of your things while you were asleep."

I followed him out of the bathroom.

He reached for the duffel under the chair by the bedside. He set it on the bed and unzipped it.

"Ah, do you mind?" I asked.

"Mind what?"

"Turning around."

"Sure," he said and swiveled, giving me his back.

I waited a second to make sure he really wasn't going to steal a look, and then I quickly got into the clothes he'd brought me. Jeans, a cream sweater, a pair of comfortable boots. "Okay. I'm presentable."

He turned back around and studied me from head to toe. "You're beautiful."

I wasn't an idiot. I'd seen my reflection, and I'd stared at my face with an objective eye. "Is that why you want to marry me?" I blurted out.

"No, that's not why I want to marry you," Ori said, his brown eyes softening.

He sounded genuine, and the way he was looking at me... I wasn't sure what to do with the intimacy—and desire—brewing between us. I had no memories of him, no memories of my past. I couldn't rely on him just because he was my fiancé, just because I had no one else.

Chapter 2
QUINN

"This is your home?" I asked when Ori parked the car in front of a beautiful two-story brick house with white trim.

"It is," he said. He cut the engine, and we sat for a moment before I reached for the door and got out. The sun was setting, and the temperature was dropping. Snow blanketed the lawn.

A memory flashed in my head. Winter. Sled. Red hat. My arms wrapped around a boy. The winter wind stinging my cheeks, our laughter ringing through the trees.

And just like that it was gone. I had no idea who the boy was to me, but I got the feeling that it was nothing romantic. Familiar and familial. A cousin maybe?

"Quinn?" Ori asked, coming to my side. "You okay?"

"Yeah." I nodded and then let him take my arm and guide me across the slick sidewalk. He unlocked the front door and pushed it open, gesturing for me to go inside. I hesitantly moved forward. Ori came in behind me, set the duffel down, and then shut the door.

"You want the tour?" he asked, setting his keys on the dark wood table in the foyer.

"Um. Okay."

As he showed me the house, I couldn't help but think about how I must've felt the first time I'd come here. Had he shown me the house and then made love to me in his bed? Had he held me in his arms for hours?

My breathing escalated and came out in shallow pants, and then I grew lightheaded. I stopped in my tracks to lean against a wall.

"Hey," Ori said when he realized he'd been talking to himself and that I'd fallen behind. "It's okay. Just breathe."

"I can't—"

"Don't talk." He placed a hand on my back and rubbed.

Instead of it being a comfort, it felt smothering. I shrugged my shoulders away from his touch and focused on steadying my breath. When I felt like I had it under control, I stood up and faced him.

"You okay?" he asked quietly.

I nodded.

"Want to continue on?"

"Yeah."

"Can I—can I touch you?"

I thought for a moment and then nodded. Ori took my hand and pulled me slowly against him and then wrapped his arms around me. I placed my face in the crook of his neck and closed my eyes.

"I know you think you're alone in this. I know you don't remember me, and I can't even imagine what it must be like not to remember your friends and family. But you aren't alone. I'm here. And I'll never leave you."

His words gave me pause. Never leave me? What happened if I never got my memory back? Would he stay? Would he want to create new memories with me?

"How can I not remember you?" I whispered, letting

tears fall down my cheeks. "How can I not remember loving you?"

Ori brushed his lips across my forehead. "I'll remember for the both of us." Somehow, he managed to hold me even tighter.

I breathed him in, memorizing the scent that clung to his skin. How often had I taken him for granted? What had our life been like? I couldn't even imagine.

Could you ever really have a fresh start? Did I want one?

Pulling out of his arms, I didn't go far. I grasped his hand, and with bravado I didn't feel, I said, "Show me the rest of the house."

"Later," he said, bringing our clasped hands to his lips. "I'm hungry."

As if on cue, my stomach rumbled, causing me to laugh. "So am I, apparently."

"I'm cooking you dinner."

"You cook?" I asked in surprise.

"I do." He led me back downstairs. "For the record, you don't."

"I don't cook? Are you sure you're not marrying me just because I'm hot?" I teased, trying to lighten the mood, trying to focus on anything resembling normal.

"I promise I'm not marrying you just because you're hot."

"How did we meet?"

Ori gestured for me to take a seat at the kitchen table. I traced a wood grain with my pointer finger as I waited for him to answer.

"I was an asshole," he said and opened a cabinet to pull out a pot. "The night we met, I mean."

"You're really selling yourself."

He laughed and then told me the story of how we met at the mayor's gala.

I shook my head. "Mayor? Why was I at the mayor's gala?"

"Ah, your family is very prominent in Boston society."

"Oh God, was I a debutante?"

"No," he hastened to assure me. "Not like that. Just—you come from a wealthy, influential family."

"I do?"

He sighed. "I know you want to know everything right away, but trust me when I say not to ask anything more about your family tonight. Okay?"

I took a deep breath. "Okay."

"Okay?" he repeated.

Nodding, I gestured to the ingredients he was assembling. "What are you making?"

"Lamb chops."

My mouth watered at the thought. Guess I wasn't a vegetarian.

"Now, normally, I would pour you a glass of wine and let you sit there and entertain me, but the doctor said you should limit your alcohol and sugar intake. It's supposed to help with brain function."

"No wine with lamb?" I asked. "Doesn't that seem sort of…sacrilegious?"

Ori smiled. "Definitely."

"Well, now that I can't drink, can I be your sous-chef?"

Chapter 3
QUINN

Ori lit candles and dimmed the lights. It was romantic and sweet—and the food was delicious.

"Well, now I know why I said yes to your proposal," I teased, pushing away my empty plate. He chuckled and reached for my hand. I let him. "I'm nervous, Ori."

"About what?"

"Sharing a bed with you."

"I'll sleep in the guest room. Until you're ready. Whatever you need, Quinn."

Relief curled through my belly, and I nodded. "It's weird, you know?"

"I know."

We sat in silence for a moment, and then I stood up and grabbed our plates, planning to take them to the sink, but Ori's hand on my arm stopped me. "Leave it. I'll take care of it."

"You sure?"

He nodded. "Why don't you head upstairs and take a hot shower."

"Are you saying I smell like a hospital?"

"I'm saying take some time to yourself. I know you want it."

I set the plates back on the table and then leaned over to brush my lips across his. "Thank you. Thank you for dinner and just—thank you."

He smiled. "It was my pleasure." Ori let go of my arm.

I wandered out of the kitchen. My hand trailed up the wood bannister as I climbed the stairs. There were no adornments, no framed photographs on the walls. Not even one of us as a couple. Come to think of it, I hadn't seen any photographs in the living room either. I made a note to ask Ori about it after my shower.

There was a guest bathroom on the way to the master bedroom, and I ducked in there. I wasn't quite ready to shower in the bathroom I'd shared with Ori. I wasn't ready to see elements of him in the bathroom—his toothbrush, his shaving cream. Maybe I wasn't ready to see how our personal touches twined together. Intimacy wasn't something that could be forced, and at the moment, I didn't need a reminder of what I couldn't remember.

I closed the guest bathroom door and leaned against it for a moment. A linen closet off to the side held a set of gray towels. They were soft to the touch and looked fairly new. I took the biggest one and hung it on the hook next to the shower.

I shed my clothes and stared at myself in the mirror. My eyes lingered on my breasts and then slid down my belly. Frowning, I peered closer as my fingers traced the thin light scars that marred the skin of my lower stomach.

My breath hitched, and I sank to the floor as the memory came to me.

I was standing in front of a gray headstone with a modest cross. I was underneath a black umbrella, holding onto a man who wore a dark suit.

Grief welled up inside of me, and I cried out in anguish.

I'd had a baby and lost it.

Who was the man next to me? The baby's father?

I felt a hand on my shoulder. "What happened? Quinn?"

"Remembered…something…" I whispered through broken breaths, not caring that he was here and intruding on a deeply personal moment. My head rested on my knees, and I refused to look at Ori.

I felt him move behind me, and he sat, gathering me to him. He wrapped his arms around me so I was pressed against his chest.

"Tell me," he said, voice low, undemanding.

"Did we…" I inhaled a shaky breath. "Did we lose a baby?"

Ori brushed the hair away from my nape and placed a gentle kiss against my skin. "No, Quinn. We didn't lose a baby."

"But I did lose one…didn't I?"

"Yes." His voice was full of pain—pain for me.

I dissolved into a mess of tears and tried to curl myself into the tightest ball imaginable. I'd had a baby and lost it. It hadn't been with Ori. That was all I knew. I cried for my loss and the missing puzzle pieces.

When I felt my emotions calm, I eased out of Ori's embrace. Embarrassment washed over me when I realized I was naked. Naked and sitting on the floor with dried tears staining my cheeks.

"If it wasn't ours, whose was it?"

He paused. "The man before me."

I tried to picture him—the man that came before Ori. Of course I couldn't see a thing. Black. A gaping hole of blackness.

"I'm okay now," I lied.

"All right." Ori made no move to get up.

"Seriously."

"I believe you."

"No, you don't." I pulled my knees closer to my chest. Ori traced my shoulder blade and then trailed down my spine. I shivered. "Please, don't."

His hand dropped from my skin, and then there was a draft of cool air against my back. I heard the door open and then close.

It took me a moment to peel myself off the floor. I turned on the shower and waited for the room to fill with steam and kept my eyes from seeking out my reflection in the mirror.

With each question came many more.

I'd almost had a baby with a man—a man who was not my current fiancé. Had I been married before? Was I divorced? A widow?

I glanced at my left hand. My ring finger was bare. There was no engagement ring. Something else I needed to ask Ori about.

I took my time in the shower. Maybe I was hiding, maybe I was delaying asking Ori questions he didn't want to answer. Or refused to.

It was a good sign, though, that I'd started to have flashes of memories. Wasn't it? That surely meant I'd remember it all—my life before. What happened when I did? Would I wish for oblivion? Or would I be completely overjoyed that I could remember Ori and our relationship?

As I toweled off, I tried to think about him objectively. He'd sat by my bedside in the hospital. He'd held me while I'd fallen apart. He wasn't pushing me into being physical with him in any way.

His actions showed he was a good man.

And yet…something was missing, and not just my memory. There was a niggling sensation, a tickle, at the back of my mind. It wasn't telling me not to trust Ori, but it was telling me to be careful.

To look beneath his words and his actions.

I wrapped the towel around me and opened the bathroom door. Steam swirled out into the hallway and dissipated. I went to the master bedroom and stood in the middle of the floor. There was a dresser against one gray wall. I went to it and pulled open the top drawer.

Ori's underwear.

The next dresser drawer housed his socks. Then undershirts. Then jeans.

No clothing of mine.

"Ori!" I called. I waited a few moments and then heard his footsteps on the stairs. I turned to look at him. His gaze was on my face, and then it dipped lower. I swallowed. "Um. I can't find my clothes."

He sighed. "You don't have any clothes here."

I frowned. "I don't?"

"No."

"I don't even have a drawer?"

"I tried to give you a drawer. You refused."

"*I* refused."

He nodded, a slight smile on his face. "You were determined to keep your independence."

"Is that why I'm not wearing an engagement ring?"

Instead of replying, he went to a bedside table—the one on the right side—opened the drawer and pulled out a black velvet ring box. He walked over and held it out to me. "I had to get it resized."

I looked at the ring box but made no move to take it.

"What's the matter?" Ori teased. "You scared? It's just a ring. Your ring."

"Did I like it?" I asked faintly.

"Just open it," he said, voice low.

With a deep inhale, I took the box. "Oh," I breathed when I saw it, the beauty of the ring literally taking my breath away.

"The ring belonged to my grandmother," he said. "Three carat European cut."

"It's beautiful."

We both fell silent. Ori watched me as I studied the fine piece of jewelry. Finally, he asked, "Do you want to wear it?"

I opened my mouth to speak but found I couldn't. Instead, I nodded. With great reverence, Ori took the ring box from me. He removed the ring, lifted my hand, and slid the diamond onto my finger. He pressed a kiss to the back of my hand and then gave it a squeeze.

"Ori?"

"Hmmm?"

"I really do need some clothes."

Chapter 4

SASHA

The Manhattan warehouse apartment I'd once shared with Quinn was littered with the remains of her anger. I immediately adjusted the thermostat. It had been kept at fifty in my absence. For some reason, Dimitri had insisted on it despite my assurance I'd never return to New York.

Apparently, he'd known better.

Quinn.

When I thought of her, I ached. I ached deep in my gut. So I hadn't thought of her this past year. Couldn't think about her. Because if I'd thought about her, then I'd have to remember I was a coward. A fucking coward who'd walked out on a woman who'd not only sat by my bedside while my burnt flesh healed but had loved me through it.

I hadn't deserved her.

She deserved a hero. A whole man.

I was gruesome. Ugly. Blind in one eye.

Quinn was beautiful. Stunning. Strong yet soft. She was everything I hadn't been looking for. Hadn't known I'd needed.

After Barrett…

God, Barrett.

That woman had fucked me up.

Everything in my place was covered in a layer of dust. Apparently, Dimitri didn't think to hire someone to keep it clean while I was gone. Hence, the broken glass and the cobwebs in the corners of the ceilings. I turned on all the water valves. The apartment eventually warmed, and I finally shrugged out of my coat. I hadn't traveled with any bags, but all my clothes were still in the closet. So were Quinn's. From what I could tell, she'd taken nothing when she left.

I knew she was in Boston. I knew I was an ass for leaving her.

I scrubbed a hand across the right side of my face. Reconstruction had only done so much, but at least now I didn't look like a comic book villain. But half my face was noticeably scarred, rough to the touch.

I'd left New York nearly a year ago with no plan to return. I'd bled on its streets, I'd sacrificed, I'd killed, I'd captured. I'd lost myself. I'd found myself. I'd fallen in love. I'd failed at love.

I'd become a man here.

New York summoned me.

I pulled out my cell and called Dimitri. He answered on the first ring. "I'm back," I said without preamble.

There was a moment of silence, and then he replied, "Good."

"*Krasnyy?*"

"Already here."

"See you in twenty."

∾

Krasnyy was my creation. From the catacomb-inspired walls to the hidden entrance and the smeared painted sign, patrons weren't sure what they were going to get when they stepped into my bar. It was for the elite. Dark. With a seedy undertone. It was everything I had ever envisioned for myself. I came from nothing. Less than nothing. Some of it I'd earned. Some of it I'd taken.

The bartender was in the middle of talking to a customer, but his eyes lifted and rested on me. His mouth gaped open and then it shut.

The king has returned, I thought morosely. It would be interesting to see how my absence had affected my men. I wondered if I would have to make another play for power since technically, I'd handed everything over to Dimitri and left the country. Did I even want to challenge for power?

Dimitri sat in the farthest booth in the corner, facing the exit. His gaze remained steady as I approached the table. I stood there for a moment. Finally, Dimitri climbed out of the booth and embraced me.

"Good to have you back, *brat*." He grinned and moved aside so I could take his seat.

"It's good to be back," I admitted in Russian, sliding across expensive suede. Suede was a bitch to clean but well worth it.

"You're uglier since the last time I saw you."

I let out a laugh, a sharp crack of noise that reverberated through the bar and turned heads. "Ugly is in the eye of the beholder."

Dimitri smirked. "I'm pretty sure that's not how the saying goes."

I ran a hand across the right side of my head where blond hair wouldn't grow back. I wore the rest of it sheared close to my skull. I avoided mirrors.

"Where do you want to start?" Dimitri asked.

"Territory?"

"Three percent growth. We've diversified our holdings."

"Good."

"*Krasnyy* is at capacity every night. Expansion of *Krasnyy* vodka is underway as is the new ad campaign. I had to fire the agency and take our account somewhere else. They were giving shit ideas. No innovation."

Mention of the ad campaign made me think of Quinn. The famous *Krasnyy* girl. She'd sat in a vat of vodka, the sexiest damn look on her face while a photographer snapped photo after photo of her.

"Sasha," Dimitri said.

"Yeah?" I asked, coming back to the present.

"She's fine."

I swallowed the questions. I wanted to know everything about Quinn that I'd missed, everything I'd walked away from. Which was why I shouldn't ask. I didn't deserve to know. I had no right. Yet I couldn't stop myself from wanting to soak up every scrap of information that pertained to her.

"You know this how?"

Dimitri paused. "I've been checking in with her. She told me not to."

"Sounds like Quinn." I smiled and then it slipped. What the hell did I know about her? It had been a year. A lot could happen in a year.

"She's just now getting back on her feet," Dimitri said. "Her father died—"

"Michael died?" I interrupted. "When?"

"Couple of months ago."

I leaned back in the booth. Her father had died, and I hadn't been there for her. "How?"

"Cancer. Pancreatic. Fast."

If it was possible, I felt like an even bigger shit.

I'd known Michael O'Malley. Respected him. We'd done business together. And when O'Malley wanted retribution against the Italians who'd kidnapped Quinn, we'd become family. I'd have gone after them myself, but at the time, I'd been nearly dead in the hospital.

Quinn had been bait—bait to draw me out. Those bastards had gone after my woman to get to me. Fucking cowards. They'd paid, but unfortunately, revenge hadn't wiped away their stain. Their actions lingered, like a greasy oil stain on cement.

"Why?" Dimitri asked quietly.

"Because I was ready," I stated. "I was ready to come back to New York."

"What about Quinn?"

"What about her?"

"Are you planning on reconciling?"

My eyes hardened. Dimitri was my trusted second. He'd been running things since I'd left. But that didn't mean I'd open my mouth, spill my heart onto the table. There were some things I didn't discuss. Not even with Dimitri.

"How did you feel in the leader position?" I asked instead of answering him.

"Good."

"And the men? Did they have a hard time adjusting?"

"They…missed you. But we made do. Are you ready to take your place again?"

"That's not why I came back," I said. "I'm not here to challenge you for the leadership role. I gave it to you. Everyone has adjusted. They've dealt with enough change."

Dimitri frowned. "If you don't want the leadership role, then what do you want?"

A sardonic smile curved my lips. "Hell if I know."

Chapter 5

QUINN

My eyes opened, and I encountered darkness. Ori's deep breathing was a strange sort of comfort. Comforting because he was another human being, and I didn't feel so alone. But it had nothing to do with my relationship with him.

When we'd gotten ready for bed, I'd asked him to sleep next to me. It had seemed like the right thing to do.

My right hand rested on my left. I traced the diamond ring which fit snugly against my knuckle. It felt like anything but a comfort. I wasn't sure how to feel about it, actually.

What had woken me up? A sound? No. A dream. Smoky fragments of it teased the corners of my memory, begging to return. The door of my mind stayed firmly shut.

A warm hand reached out and grazed my leg. It squeezed my thigh and then let go. I waited for Ori to tell me he was awake, but all he did was sigh in his sleep.

I looked at the alarm clock; it was just past four in the

morning. I gently eased out of bed, not wanting to wake Ori.

When I got downstairs to the living room, I took a blanket and wrapped it around me. The house was warm, but I wanted to be encased, snuggled up in something soft. I was wearing Ori's pajamas. The flannel pants were too long, and the long-sleeved thermal was too big, but I didn't have my own clothes.

Why didn't I have my own clothes at my fiancé's house?

Some things just weren't making sense to me.

I didn't need all my memories to know that a feeling in my gut was telling me things were wrong. Off.

Things I knew to be true.

I am Quinn O'Malley.

I was in a car accident.

I lost a baby.

People lied. My body didn't. There was evidence that I'd carried a child, and I'd been far enough along to show.

What did I do with that? Tuck it away, hoard it like a missing puzzle piece and hope the rest of it came together? I had to rely on Ori to tell me when he thought I was ready to hear. I wanted my memories back, and I wanted them back now. I'd insist on it. And maybe he would only feed me slivers, until I remembered everything.

"Quinn?"

I started and turned my head. Ori stood in the doorway of the living room, his dark hair mussed, exhaustion at the creases of his eyes. "Did I wake you?" I asked.

He shook his head and came into the living room to sit on the couch next to me. "How could you wake me? You haven't made a sound."

"Then why are you awake?"

"Rolled over and felt you weren't there. What's wrong?"

"Nothing."

He didn't prod me into talking. Seemed like he knew better.

"Can I sit here with you?"

"On one condition. You tell me something. About my past," I clarified.

Leaning back against the couch, Ori looked thoughtful. "You have a best friend you've known since you were five."

I blinked. "I do?"

He nodded.

"Why haven't I seen her?" I demanded.

Ori sighed. "I called her. From the waiting room. She knows you were in an accident. She knows you lost your memory. And she also knows what the doctor said about you remembering too fast."

"And you and the doctor both think my best friend will spill everything and my mind will break, and I'll be broken forever."

"Can't you have a little patience?"

"What would you do if it were you, Ori?" I demanded. "Have patience? What if you didn't remember me?" I held my hand up and pointed to the engagement ring. "Do you know what this means? This means we had a life together, and I don't remember it. I don't remember you, my love for you. And what if all it takes is seeing someone else, talking to someone else, and it'll all come back for me."

"What if it doesn't?" he shot back. "What if you see Shannon? What if she tells you all about your high school days? What if she tells you about the boys you've loved and whose hearts you've broken? And it doesn't matter and you still don't remember."

"Can *you* tell me about the baby I've lost?"

He flinched like I'd hit him.

"I didn't think so." I scooted away from him, not wanting to be in his space. Not wanting to look at him.

Ori got up and went to the mantle. "Your phone," he said, picking it up and bringing it to me. "It's locked. I don't know the password." He tossed it, and it landed on the couch. "You remember the password, then you have access to all your photos. All your emails. Everything.

"You open that phone, you can call your best friend and tell her you remember. Until then," he shrugged, "I'm with the doctor. It'll come back in due time."

"Or it won't," I said.

"You don't really believe that." He peered at me. "You're having flashes, aren't you? Of your memories."

I closed my mouth, wanting to hoard them. So far Ori hadn't been in any of them. I wasn't cruel enough to tell him that not only could I not remember our life together, but it seemed my brain was in no hurry to remember him.

Chapter 6
SASHA

It was my first night in Manhattan, and I didn't sleep. Instead, I walked the streets. A few men who thought I was an easy mark quickly learned I was darker than the shadows. More deadly too, even though they had blades, and I had nothing except my fists and a lot of anger.

I'd abandoned Quinn. But I did it for me as much as I did it for her. I'd done her a kindness. I hadn't been strong enough, physically or mentally. I hadn't been the man she'd met or fallen in love with. I'd become weak.

Self-loathing filled my throat, the burn of rage choking me.

But I'd done enough wallowing the year I'd been gone. And there was no going back to change my actions. Not that I was sure I'd change them anyhow.

As I walked in four-hundred-dollar Italian leather shoes, the sun finally rose, bathing the gritty, dirty streets of Manhattan in golden light. I found myself in front of The Rex Hotel.

I hadn't talked to Barrett in months. The last time we

spoke, I'd told her I was going to Russia. It hadn't been a lie.

Before I could think better of it, I nodded to one of the doormen who opened the doors for me. To his credit, he didn't flinch when he saw my face. I strode in and immediately felt comfortable. I'd spent enough time in this hotel. Countless meetings in the penthouse suite and in the restaurant. So many hours plotting, devising. Forming allies, destroying friendships, surging new business partnerships.

The lobby elevator doors dinged open, and the woman I'd once been in love with walked across the marble floor. Her auburn hair was up, pinned away from her face, showing off her cheekbones. She looked elegant in gray wool slacks and a black cashmere sweater.

A desk agent called out a greeting, and she replied with a call of her own. Barrett's gaze slid from the woman, a smile still on her face. When her eyes locked with mine, her grin slipped, and she stopped.

Her lips formed my name, but no sound came out. "Sasha!" she yelled. She ran toward me, without concern that she'd shattered her hip in an accident. She stumbled, but before she could hit the floor, I was there, dragging her into my arms.

I closed my eyes as I breathed her in. She smelled like vanilla and the wax crayons her children colored with.

She pulled out of my arms, her eyes searching my face. I watched her take in the changes—the healed skin that would never be normal.

"You're back," she whispered.

"I am."

"Good." And then she decked me. A stream of curses passed her lips as she shook out her hand. "Jesus, that always looks cooler in the movies."

My jaw throbbed where she'd clocked me. "If it makes you feel any better, I know I'm going to have a bruise."

"Serves you right, you bastard," she said, but then she smiled, taking the sting out of her insult. "What the hell are you doing here?"

"I thought you were happy to see me," I teased with a grin. Wincing, my smile slipped. There was no need to inflate Barrett's ego; I hadn't lied—my jaw fucking hurt.

"I am happy to see you. Relieved too. You're not dead."

It was said lightly, but in our world, silence from a friend meant one of two things: either you were underground and running from the law, or one of your enemies had managed to kill you.

"Where's Campbell?" I asked.

"Meeting."

"What about you? Were you headed out?"

She shook her head. "I was coming down to have breakfast. Join me."

It was not a request. In the handful of years that Barrett had been married to Campbell, she'd learned how to command with the authority of a queen.

I followed her to the bar and restaurant. With a quick smile, Barrett passed the young hostess. The woman looked at me, her greeting dying on her lips.

New York was such an odd place. No one batted an eye when someone walked a bunny rabbit on a leash, but a badly burned guy? People didn't know what to do.

Barrett settled into her favorite booth—the one always kept open even if she and Campbell were in Scotland. She took the black linen napkin, shook it out, and placed it in her lap. "You have good timing. In another few hours, you would have missed us."

"I didn't know I was coming here."

She didn't reply as she studied me, marking the changes. "You healed better than I expected. Did you have surgery while you were gone?"

I shrugged.

"That's not an answer."

"What else do you notice?" I wanted to know what she saw.

"You look…sharper. Harder. Guess you haven't been withering away in that cold barren wasteland you call home."

"I don't call Russia home."

"Then why did you go there?"

Our conversation fell silent when the waiter approached our table. He poured a bottle of sparkling water while Barrett ordered. Then the waiter looked at me. "Sir? Do you need a menu?"

"I'll have the same as the lady," I said, not taking my eyes off her. When we were alone again, I picked up the thread of our conversation. "I was only in Russia for a few weeks."

She blinked. "A few weeks? Where have you been all this time?"

I hesitated, finding it difficult to carry on a conversation after so many months of solitude. But I found I wanted to confide in Barrett. She'd always been easy to confide in.

"I was in Japan."

Surprise registered on her face. "Japan? Why?"

I wanted to reach out and touch my water glass but knew it was a nervous tick, so I forced my hand to stay where it was, relaxed and on the table.

"I was badly broken—not just my body, but my mind too," I said, pitching my voice lower. Though there were only a few tables with patrons due to the early hour, I felt no need for them to hear about my wandering journey.

"I knew I was never going to be the same man again. I wanted to become stronger. So I went to Japan and trained in the arts of the ancient Samurai."

I waited for her to laugh, but instead, she merely nodded, so I continued.

"I'm not sure how I survived," I admitted. "They're rigorous, brutal. I learned martial arts. How to wield a sword and a bow and arrow."

I also knew how to do those things on the back of a horse. Not sure I'd ever need that skill, but it was part of the training.

"Why?" she asked, clearly not understanding why I'd chosen an ancient study.

"Acuity. I had to"—I searched for the words— "learn a new way of thinking, of being, of living. I had to become a warrior, Barrett."

"Guess that explains why you're so cut."

I finally grinned, not even caring that the stretching of my brutalized skin might be terrifying. "I was cut before," I reminded her.

Barrett stood up and leaned over to place her hand on my scarred cheek. "I'm glad you're back," she said again.

I set my hand on top of hers and held it there. Our moment was interrupted by the return of the waiter with our two coffees. Barrett's hand dropped from my cheek. The waiter glanced between us, obviously curious. He quietly disappeared, leaving us alone again.

"Think he's going to call Campbell and tell him his wife was touching another man?" I asked lightly.

"God, I hope so," she said with a scrunch of her nose. "I'd give anything for him to come storming in here and then see his reaction when he realizes it's you."

I let out a laugh. "You torment your husband."

"He torments himself," she replied with a wave of her hand. She reached for the creamer and poured a healthy dose into her black coffee. White swirled and then became caramel.

"Flynn is aware of what I have done for him. He's… made his peace with it. With my past. With our past," she clarified.

"If you think that, then you really don't know your husband at all," I pointed out.

"Scared for your hide, Sasha?"

"If Campbell had wanted me dead, it would've happened a long time ago."

Barrett tapped the rim of her coffee cup as she thought. "I did expect a blood bath. After Dolinsky."

"Let's not talk about Dolinsky," I said.

Igor Dolinsky, the ghost that bound us all together.

She took a sip of her coffee and then set her cup down. "So tell me." She leaned forward, hazel eyes sparking with fire. "Can you teach me some bad-ass Samurai moves?"

Chapter 7
SASHA

"It's not like I'm extremely proficient," I said, finally reaching for my own cup of coffee. I didn't put anything in it, choosing to drink the strong brew black.

"Wait, wait, wait," she said. "You're not proficient? What was all this warrior talk?"

"I said I wasn't *extremely* proficient. You can't study for a few months and call yourself an expert."

"True," she allowed. "You wouldn't by any chance be trying to get out of showing me things, would you?"

"Aren't you on your way back to Scotland later today?"

"Semantics."

"Logistics," I said with a laugh.

Barrett leaned back in the booth and stared at me. "Do you know how long it's been since I've heard you laugh? It looks good on you."

"I'm not the same man I was."

"You are who you choose to be."

"That sounds very old and wise."

"Old? Who the hell are you calling old?" she demanded, raising auburn eyebrows.

"Are you about to throw down?"

"Hmmm. No." She smiled. "I've mellowed with age."

"I'm not going to say anything about your age."

The waiter brought our food, cracked some black pepper, and then left. I broke the poached egg over a perfectly toasted English muffin. I took a bite. "The food has gotten better."

"Better? Better than what?" she demanded, her own fork halfway to her mouth.

I grinned.

"Jerk," she huffed on a laugh. Then she shook her head and sobered. "I hated that you left."

"You know why I had to do it, though. Don't you?"

She nodded.

"Quinn wouldn't have understood," I murmured.

Saying her name out loud to Barrett was a knife in my ribs.

"How do you know? You never gave her the chance. You just *left*."

"It was better that way."

"If you believe that," she muttered. She went back to eating and then stopped again. "You hurt her. Not just because you left, but how you left."

"It would've been easier if I'd died. It's your fault I didn't," I reminded her.

She rolled her eyes. "How long are you going to lord that over me? I tried, Sasha. It wasn't my fault that Flynn was two steps ahead of both of us."

"Say it, Barrett. Say what you want to say."

"Coward." The word had no heat, but I felt its burn anyway. "You're a coward, Sasha Petrovich. And it doesn't matter what you say, about why you left, how you left, because you left the woman you loved, who loved you through it all."

"I didn't want her pity," I said through a clenched jaw.

"She didn't ever pity you, you idiot." Barrett shook her head. "I guess I never told you about my conversation with Quinn when you were both in the hospital. The drugs were working their way out of her system and you were—well, we knew what had happened to you and what we expected.

"I told her the accident would change you. That you wouldn't be the same man she'd known and maybe it was better if she left."

Blood rushed to my head.

"She obviously didn't listen to me because she stayed with you through that year when you were healing. When I was healing." She shook her head, lost in a moment of her own past, her own trauma.

"What did she say, Barrett?"

"She told me to go fuck myself. Well, in Quinn language anyway." She smiled softly. "That's how I knew she was going to be okay…with however it played out. If you died or if you lived, I knew Quinn was going to be okay. But then you left her, and I wanted to kill you with my own two hands because *that* was something none of us expected."

Barrett picked up her cup of coffee and brought it to her lips yet didn't drink. "Is that why you came back? For her?"

"Don't you think I'd be in Boston if that was my intention?"

"You daft prick."

"She wouldn't forgive me anyway."

Barrett opened her mouth to say something but thought better of it.

"What?"

"Not my place."

I snorted. "That logic doesn't apply to us. It's never applied to us."

"I know," she said, her voice tinged with a faraway memory. "I think about him, you know. Every day."

"I do too," I admitted. "Do you still dream about him?"

Barrett nodded. "Not as much anymore. Thankfully. But yes. I still have dreams."

"My dreams are nightmares."

"If there's a hell," Barrett said with a sigh, "then we're surely going there."

"Are you sure it's that black and white?"

"Most of life isn't. But what we did to Igor Dolinsky…" She didn't go on. Couldn't maybe. "I know why I did it. Do you?"

Igor Dolinsky had been my best friend and my leader. Before me, he'd led the Russian mob. Years ago, when he'd kidnapped Barrett, he'd set off a chain reaction that still had consequences. With my help, Barrett had shot Igor. She'd gone back to Flynn. I'd taken over the Russian territories. And Barrett and I were now forever linked because of what we'd both endured at Igor Dolinsky's hands.

"You know what it's like," I said, my voice pitched low, "to feel… itchy…in your own skin."

"I know," she said. "But I stayed. I stayed with Flynn anyway."

"You're a woman. You don't know what it's like for a man to be less than a man."

"Quinn never saw you that way. And neither did I for that matter."

"It was never about you or Quinn," I finally snapped. "Don't you see, Barrett? None of that mattered. *I* mattered. What I thought of myself mattered. I had to discover who I was without all of you clawing at me. I couldn't worry about Quinn, and I knew, *I knew*, that if I'd stayed, she would've resented me. And I would've resented her. Because she's so fucking good, Barrett. She would've loved me through my brokenness, hoping it healed me. And in doing so, that would've broken her too."

Her hazel eyes trained on me, searching, seeking.

"I wasn't going to let her sacrifice herself for a man who no longer existed. Can't you understand that?" I injected a note of pleading into my tone, begging this woman whose soul was twined with mine. Because Barrett and I were forged in the fire. We'd done things—terrible things—things neither us admitted in the daytime. Our confessions were offered under the blanket of darkness, armed with vodka which loosened our tongues.

When it was clear Barrett wasn't going to reply, I went on. "Quinn won't take me back. And frankly, I don't blame her."

"Don't know until you try. Unless you don't want her. Unless…" She grinned wickedly. "Unless you're afraid, Sasha Petrovich."

"Questioning my manhood, Barrett Campbell?"

She leaned back. "My job as your best friend, wouldn't you say?"

"You're not my best friend."

She raised her eyebrows. "I'm not?"

I smiled. "There's not a word for what you are to me, Barrett. And you know that."

Chapter 8
QUINN

"I'm an amnesiac, not an invalid," I said, my hands holding the cup of coffee like it was a lifeline. "Staying inside is not going to do anything to help me. In fact, I'll probably go nuts. You don't want me to go nuts, do you?"

Ori picked up the spatula and flipped the fried egg in the ceramic pan. "Did you unlock your phone?" he asked without looking at me.

"No." Instead of going back to bed last night, I'd sat up, holding my phone in my hand and pressing number combinations until my fingers were tired.

I was on my second cup of coffee, all on an empty stomach. The last thing I needed was an ulcer on top of amnesia. Ori turned off the burner, lifted the pan, and the eggs slid off onto the waiting plate. He placed a few slices of bacon next to the eggs and brought the plate to me.

"Thank you," I said, picking up my fork.

"What do you want me to do? Drive you around town to some of your favorite spots hoping it'll jar something loose?"

I looked at him. His eyes were tired, and his mouth was

lined with exhaustion. "I'm sorry," I said quietly. "I haven't been thinking about how bad this is for you."

He shook his head. "I'm not taking anything personally. Believe me."

"I feel like a raging bitch. Was I a raging bitch before I lost my memory?"

Ori smiled. "You do realize there's no good way to answer that, right?"

I laughed.

"Eat before it gets cold." Ori went back to the stove and turned on the burner again. "I'll drive you around, if you want. But I don't know what good that will do."

"You could call Shannon," I suggested after taking a slice of bacon and biting off a good amount. "You could have her take me around. Maybe it will help if I spend time with someone I've known forever."

Ori didn't say anything as he cracked an egg into the pan. Finally, he said, "All right."

"Really?" I asked in disbelief.

"Yeah, really." He sighed. "I shouldn't keep you here just because I want to protect you."

"Protect me from what?" I asked.

"Everything, Quinn. I'm trying to protect you from everything."

I looked at his wide shoulders. They were strong. He was strong. I'd been pressed up against his chest and felt the strength of his arms around me.

"You know what I'd like to do instead?" I asked.

"What's that?" He still wouldn't look at me.

"I think I'd like to go get my clothes. Look around the apartment I was so determined to keep as mine, and move my stuff in."

"Quinn, you don't have to—"

"And I hope I'm one of those women who has a

gorgeous dress and high heels in her closet because I want to take you out to dinner."

"You don't have to do that."

"I want to."

"You sure?" He looked at me, vulnerability etched across his face.

My heart ached for him. This wasn't something we were ever supposed to have to go through. We were young and in love. Forgetting the one you loved was enough of a worry when you got old. But this? Now?

No.

"I want to remember you," I whispered. "More than anything."

A smile crept across his face. "You're not taking me out to dinner. I'm taking *you* out to dinner."

"But first let's get my clothes."

"Probably for the best," he said. The eggs finished cooking, and he put them on his plate. "As much as I love seeing you in my clothes, can't say they fit you that well."

I grinned. "That was a polite way of saying I look dumpy."

"There you go, putting words into my mouth again." He brought his plate to the table and sat down next to me. "I think it will be nice having your things here."

We ate in companionable silence for a moment before I asked, "Is this what we normally do?"

"Do?"

"For breakfast. Do you cook, and I sit and watch? Do we tease each other and then go about our day? What do you do for work? What do I do?"

"I'm begging you," he began. "Don't get caught up in the questions. The questions just bring panic, and an insane need to know what memories you're missing. Can you do me a favor? Try to be here, now. Enjoy us now even though we have a history."

"You're asking the impossible, you know. I'm going to have questions until I remember."

"I know. But try anyway." He reached out to gently tuck a strand of hair behind my ear. "It used to be long."

"What?"

"Your hair. Dark, long, down past your shoulder blades. It was beautiful. Wild. But I like the short hair too. Makes your eyes…" He shook his head and his hand dropped. "Anyway."

"See? I want more of that. That seems more real to me than filling in all the missing pieces."

"But you want those too."

"If you're willing to give them to me, then I'll take them."

"They'll mean more to you when they come back on their own."

"Are you a poet, Ori Abruzzo?" I teased, wanting to lighten the mood. He stilled, and all of a sudden his face drained of color. "Hey, I was kidding. Why do you look like that?"

"No reason." He smiled, but it looked forced. "Finish your breakfast and then let's get your stuff."

Ori dropped the keys onto the foyer table as I stepped into the living room. Or what could be considered a living room. It was small. And at the moment, there was a large wooden desk in the corner and an antique liquor cart with a crystal decanter and matching glasses.

"This is my apartment?" I asked with a look at Ori.

"Yep."

I glanced around the microscopic living room and then moved down the hallway to the bedroom. It was even smaller that I could've imagined. Boxes and boxes labeled *clothes* were stacked against the wall. And a huge frilly bed took up the rest of the space.

"Are you sure I lived here?" I called out to him. "I don't have anything here!"

"Like I said, your own place for the illusion of still being independent."

I threw him a look. He stood in the doorway of the bedroom, and I placed my hands on his chest with the intention of moving him out of the way, but Ori surprised me by wrapping his arms around me and pulling me to him.

"Hi," I said.

He grinned. "Hello."

My hands slowly climbed up his chest to grasp the back of his neck. I looked up at him. My breath caught when he lowered his mouth to mine. His kiss was gentle, unhurried. Ori gripped me tighter as if to keep me from fleeing, but there was no need for that. I closed my eyes and sank into it, like a good dream you didn't want to wake from.

Ori lifted his lips from mine, but only so he could brush his mouth against my forehead. I kept my eyes closed as I buried my nose into the side of his neck.

"Quinn?"

"Hmm?"

"Was that okay?"

I nodded but didn't say anything. The kiss had been wonderful. New. For me anyway. I waited for the feeling of panic, but there was none. Eventually, I stepped away. Meeting his gaze, I smiled and then reached out to touch his cheek. He turned his mouth and kissed my palm.

I suddenly remembered something. Another man had

done the same thing. Kissed my palm and looked at me with naked vulnerability.

My hand dropped from Ori's cheek as I inhaled a sharp breath.

"What is it?" Ori asked, a frown marring his face. "Are you okay?"

"Yeah," I said. "I'm fine." I forced a bright smile. He studied me for a moment but didn't push. I finally moved past him and headed to the bathroom. My toiletries were sitting on the counter of the tiny sink. I opened the medicine cabinet. The shelves were full of makeup.

I liked makeup.

Which meant there was a strong possibility that I also liked shoes.

"I guess I'm a girly girl, huh?"

"Yeah, you are." His tone was tinged with amusement. "It's a good thing."

"It is what it is. So how do you want to do this?" I asked.

"Do what?"

"I don't own a lot, which seems weird. Just clothes and some antique furniture."

"I can call a few guys. Have it all moved to the house today."

I nodded. "Okay." I looked around the bathroom. It was barely big enough for one person, let alone two. The shower was narrow. At least it was bright and clean.

"I thought there would be *more*."

"More stuff?" Ori asked.

I shook my head and started pulling out tubes of lipstick and mascara from the medicine cabinet, only to realize I didn't have a box to put them in. "More familiarity—that this was a place I'd recognize. But none of it is jarring anything loose."

"You only got this apartment about a week ago, Quinn."

"A week?" I asked in confusion. "Where was I living before?"

"At the house you grew up in."

I blinked. And then I blinked again. "I was *living* with my parents?" I frowned. "No, that can't be right. In the hospital, you told me I'd lost both of them…"

"You lost your mom when you were a teenager."

"And my dad?" I asked, feeling the confusion continue to grow. "What happened to my dad?"

"Fuck it," he growled. "I can't handle the secrecy. Every question begets a question. Your father passed away recently. It wasn't sudden. He was sick. You took care of him."

Dizziness assaulted me followed by nausea. I reached out to grip the edge of the sink. "How recent?"

His eyes were sad when he answered. "A few months ago."

"How's my godson?" I asked, finishing off my breakfast.

Barrett smiled up at the waiter who came by to clear our plates. She held the cup of lukewarm coffee between her hands as she said, "Turning my hair gray."

I laughed. "Yeah, right."

"Okay. Metaphorically gray. Not actually gray. He asks about you."

Barrett's three boys were close in age and little monsters. Adorable monsters that were challenging on a good day. A spark of jealousy that I didn't have a family ignited in my belly.

"I'll come for a visit soon," I said, my voice gruff.

"And make sure you bring presents."

"For you or for them?"

Barrett smiled, and then her gaze drifted away from me to look over my shoulder. Her smile brightened. I turned and saw the reason for it.

Flynn Campbell prowled into the bar and restaurant. His strides were long and filled with purpose.

If there had been any man to lose Barrett to, Campbell

was the one. He was a good man and had somehow come to grips with my odd relationship with his wife. I stood up and went to intercept him, my hand outstretched.

Campbell grasped it, and we shook, a grin spreading across his face. "You bastard. Damn good to see you." He slapped me on the back with his free hand.

I laughed. "Good to see you, too."

Campbell's gaze darted to Barrett. "Hen," he greeted. "You didn't think to warn me he was coming back?"

"I didn't know, love," she answered.

We headed back to the table and sat down. Barrett scooted over and Campbell swallowed the space next to her. He wrapped his arm around her shoulders and kissed her. She snuggled into his embrace.

Barrett Campbell was one of the most lethal and cut-throat women in the world—but at the moment she appeared to be nothing more than a loving wife. But Campbell and I both knew what Barrett was capable of, and the things she would do for those she loved.

Had done.

The three of us had done some shady shit, all in the name of family. All in the name of love. Did that change the fact that we'd taken lives? Shed blood? Our reasons hadn't affected the consequences, just our consciences.

"Sasha?" Barrett asked.

I blinked, coming back to the conversation. Retreating from the dark corners of my mind.

"Good, just making sure you're still with us," Barrett said with a smile.

"You're back now," Campbell said, reaching for his wife's cup of coffee only to grimace when he saw how she'd doctored it. "Why do you do this to good coffee?"

"No one asked you to drink mine," she retorted. "Get your own."

"Usually a waiter is at our table the moment I walk in," Campbell pointed out. He looked around. "But it seems there are none to be found at the moment."

"Maybe if you stopped scaring the crap out of all the new kids who start working here, you'd get better service," Barrett said in dry amusement.

Campbell grinned and looked at me. "Last time we were here, I might've yelled over a menu change."

"What kind of menu change?"

"Barrett thought it would be a fun prank to have printed menus all with Scottish delicacies."

I looked at Barrett who was grinning like a kid. "You didn't."

"I did."

"Let me guess. Haggis?"

Campbell chuckled. "Aye, haggis."

"He cursed for thirty seconds in Gaelic and then yelled at the waiter to bring out the chef. The poor kid was shaking. I finally had to come clean."

"Right, and now I'm being punished for your prank. Seriously." Campbell looked around again and finally locked eyes with the hostess. She hurried over immediately and then rushed to bring him a cup of coffee.

"Well, of course *she* came to your rescue," Barrett muttered.

"She's a fetus," Campbell said automatically.

Their banter caused me to chuckle. It was nothing out of the ordinary, and it made me feel like I hadn't been gone for a year. But I had been gone for a year. Physically anyway. Mentally I'd been gone for longer—ever since I'd almost died in that fire.

The night I'd been burned had changed everything. Two years later, and it was still affecting our lives.

"So," Campbell said after taking a sip of the coffee the hostess had brought him. "What's the plan?"

"Plan? There's no plan," I said.

"You're taking over again, aye?" Campbell's brows furrowed.

"No."

"I don't understand," he said.

"I didn't come back to lead. Everything can continue on. The Russians are still in business with the Scots. Nothing has to change."

"Everything has to change," Barrett interjected. "Don Archer is retiring."

"You're kidding?" I leaned back in my seat and stretched out my legs. Don Archer was FBI. In exchange for turning a blind eye to Campbell's criminal activities, Barrett fed Archer anonymous information about other big fish. Archer had been busting crime lords for years. He'd also complained that when he took down one, three popped up in his place.

"Archer retiring is a serious problem," I said.

Barrett nodded. "Yep. Not to mention…have you been staying up to date about what's going on with the FBI?"

I shook my head. I hadn't kept up to date with anything. I'd been across the world, fighting my own battles.

"Archer doesn't even know who he can trust," Campbell said. "He says it's so corrupted that…well, anyway. He's ready to get out. Take his pension and run."

"Probably got tired of being completely ineffectual," I replied.

"No doubt," Campbell agreed. "We need someone in his place, though. Someone we can trust. Because if we don't, I might have to take the bairns and Barrett and move to an island not on the map."

"We already come to the States a lot less," Barrett said. "Trying to stay under the radar. But some business has to be taken care of in person."

There was always a risk to our lives. No matter how well armed we were, how many bodyguards, how alert, we had targets on our backs. At least I'd never spent time in prison. A few years back, Campbell had been wrongfully convicted of a crime, and it had taken Barrett weeks to get him released. She'd had to partner with the most powerful and dangerous man in Argentina to do it.

There was nothing Barrett wouldn't do for her family.

You didn't just walk away from this life. You couldn't. Blood and legacy. They seemed to go hand in hand.

"So," Campbell started, "are you going to see Quinn?"

Chapter 10
QUINN

After we left my pathetically small apartment, Ori took me to a little café for lunch. We talked about nothing over sandwiches and Italian soda. When we got back to his place, I startled in surprise to see that the few belongings I owned had made their way into his house. Including the antique desk and crystal glassware.

I hoped to remember why I'd taken those two pieces from my father's house. I hoped to remember the reason for the sentimentality.

"Am I even sentimental?" I asked my reflection as I slipped a diamond stud into my ear. It was big—over a carat. I had no idea if Ori had given the earrings to me, or if they were a family heirloom. But I'd opened my jewelry box and found only a few trinkets resting on the black velvet.

My clothes were designer, expensive. My perfume was high-end. And the bath products I used told the same story —I came from money.

It was odd to know that, to see Fendi purses in the closet next to Ori's bespoke suits.

Who was I?

Quinn O'Malley.

Teen model.

Orphan.

Childless.

Could I be considered a mother if I'd lost a late-term baby?

It was a good thing the doctor told me not to drink alcohol because it would no doubt throw me into a fit of depression—apparently, it would affect the brain—as would sugar. And if I wanted to remember, I had a better chance if I stayed clear of both.

Shaking off the threat of a somber mood, I looked at myself in the mirror. My hair was sleek and in a perfect bob, my eyelashes were long and dark, my lips red.

I smiled.

A beautiful woman smiled back at me.

Would I ever get used to my own face again?

My phone vibrated, dancing across the vanity. Shannon's name appeared on the screen. I thought about answering it but then realized I had no idea what to say to her. Having a conversation about my missing memory over the phone just didn't seem like the best idea. I silenced the phone and set it aside.

Standing up, I looked at myself one final time. When I deemed my appearance perfect, I turned and walked to the dresser to pick up my clutch. I set my tube of lipstick into one of the pockets and thought about bringing my phone. What was I going to do? Answer calls from names I didn't recognize? I set the phone back down.

"You look amazing," Ori said from behind me.

I whirled, a hand flying to my chest. "You scared me."

He grinned. "Sorry." His fingers went to button his gray suit jacket. My eyes took all of him in. Three-piece gray suit, white starched collar, cufflinks. His dark hair fell gently across his forehead, his golden skin unblemished and even.

"Do we want babies?" I blurted out.

His smile remained as he tilted his head to the side. "Babies?"

"Babies," I repeated. "We're engaged. Which means we're getting married. I just didn't know... Do we want them?"

Ori sauntered toward me until we were standing toe-to-toe. My heels put me at his nose level. His hands reached out to grasp my hips, and he pulled me close to him. So close I could smell the aftershave on his neck. So close I wanted to bury my nose against his skin.

"Yes, Quinn. We want babies."

I let out a breath, slowly, like a balloon leaking air. "I didn't know—because of what—because of the one I'd lost. I didn't know if I was ready for that again. Or if I even wanted it."

One of his hands left my hip to come up and caress my cheek, and then he grazed my lips with his. "We want babies," he whispered.

"Lots of babies?" I asked with hope.

His grin was wicked. "Lots of babies."

That sinful smile reached into my belly and released a swarm of butterflies. It made me lightheaded with desire, and I knew if we didn't get out of the bedroom, I'd ask him to take me to bed instead of dinner.

Could I go to bed with a man I didn't remember falling in love with, who promised me children and a future?

Yes. Yes, I could.

Chapter 11
QUINN

"How's the risotto?" Ori asked.

"Good," I answered. "It would be better with a glass of white. But still good."

Ori grinned. "I know what you're trying to do. It won't work."

"Guilt? You're not susceptible to guilt?"

"Not when it comes to your health. Besides, I abstained in solidarity."

"You're a king among men, Ori," I teased.

We were sitting in a booth, tucked away in the back of the restaurant. The hum of conversation reached my ears. It was all low-lit, dark wood, and romantic. Drippy candles sat in the center of the white table-clothed tables, and the brass accents of the bar gleamed.

"This feels like a first date," I said. "But not. Is that weird?"

He shook his head and reached for his glass of sparkling water. He took a sip and then set it down. His brown eyes looked darker in candlelight, and shadows caressed his cheeks.

A buzz of desire simmered in my veins. I crossed my legs.

"I know what you mean," he said, his gaze drifting to my mouth. "Everything feels new, but only because you don't remember."

Apparently, my body remembered what my mind couldn't. It wanted Ori. It wanted to feel him on top of me, sliding between my legs. It wanted pleasure and exhaustion. It wanted the taste of desire on its tongue.

Oh, yes.

My body remembered.

It remembered how good it was between us.

Maybe I was doing this all wrong. Maybe I should've been letting my body remember, and my mind would follow. Maybe my body needed to lead.

"You know one of the things I like most about you?" Ori asked mildly.

"What?"

"Your expressive face. You can't hide how you're feeling." He leaned forward, and under the table, I felt his pant leg brush against my calf. "I know what you want."

"Do you?"

He nodded slowly, his eyes dipping lower.

I shifted in my seat to give him a better view. I'd purposefully worn a black dress with a V-neck. My arms were covered and so was my back, but the dress clung. It fit like a second skin, and I felt comfortable with my body and what I wanted.

And what I wanted was Ori.

"Should I get the check?" he asked.

I nodded. I slowly rose from the table. "If you'll excuse me for a moment?" I grabbed my clutch and walked away. I asked a passing server to point me in the direction of the restroom.

Unlike the restaurant, the bathroom lighting was bright so you could see every flaw when you looked in the mirror. The older female attendant sat in a chair and smiled at me. I smiled back. A bundle of nerves settled low in my belly. My hand shook as I reapplied my lipstick. I needed just a moment to gather my thoughts.

I was about to sleep with my fiancé—and I felt as nervous as a virgin. That thought, of course, made me think about my first time and how I didn't remember it.

"Are you all right, dear?" the bathroom attendant asked.

"I'm fine, thank you." I placed the tube of lipstick back in my clutch and snapped it shut.

"Are you on a date?" she inquired with a knowing grin.

I let out a laugh. "Yeah. A first date of sorts."

"Is it going well?" The twinkle in her blue eyes was unmistakable.

"It is."

"He's a very lucky man."

"He is, isn't he?" I reached into my clutch and pulled out a twenty and dropped it in the bowl next to her. "Thank you."

I slipped out of the bathroom and felt more in control. I was just about to round the corner into the main dining room of the restaurant when I nearly ran into someone.

"I'm so sorry!" I sidestepped the redhead and continued on.

"Quinn!" the woman greeted. "Oh my God, it's been too long! It's so good to see you."

I quickly looked her over. It was like she'd stepped out of a J. Crew catalogue. Elegant, classy. With pearls around her neck. Her blue eyes raked over me, and her smile slipped.

"Listen, I know it's been a while since we've talked. Marshall and I…" She trailed off for a moment. "I heard about your father. I'm so sorry I couldn't be there for the funeral."

"Oh," I said, finally finding my voice. "Thank you."

The woman sighed. "You're mad. Of course you are."

"No, I'm not mad," I interjected. "Really, I'm not. It was good to see you." I needed to get away. I needed to get away from this woman who clearly knew me, but I didn't know her.

"Who are you here with?" she asked. "Sasha?"

My brow furrowed. "You mean Shannon?"

It was the other woman's turn to look confused. "No. Not Shannon. Sasha," she repeated. "You know, your hot Russian boyfriend?" Her eyes strayed to my left hand, and she grabbed it. "Holy crap. When did you guys get engaged?"

Nausea filled my stomach, and I was instantly light-headed. I tried to pull my hand away from her grip, but she held on.

"Quinn? Quinn!" Her palm touched my shoulder, and she pushed me back toward the direction of the bathroom. "Sit." She forced me down onto the leather chaise.

"Are you okay? Did you have the mussels? You know you shouldn't eat mussels. I know you like them, but you get sick every time."

Who the hell was this woman? And who the hell was Sasha?

Sasha.

Could he have been the man before Ori? The father of the baby I'd lost?

A swarm of black spots danced before my eyes. I slowed my breathing and focused on not passing out. The woman continued to talk. When I finally came to, I looked at her. She was sitting next to me on the leather couch.

"You okay?"

I nodded. "Yeah. Thanks." I took a deep breath. "Now do you mind telling me who the hell you are?"

Chapter 12
QUINN

The woman blinked blue eyes and then smiled. "You've always had a wicked sense of humor."

"I'm not kidding," I said. "I was in a car accident a few days ago. I hit my head, and I'm suffering from amnesia. Please." I grabbed her hand and held on tightly. "Please believe me."

Her eyes raked over my face. "Jesus, you're serious."

I nodded.

"I'm Gwen. James," she added. "We met a few years ago at a fundraiser. I'm in PR and Sasha…" She peered at me. "You remember Sasha, don't you?"

I shook my head.

"Your boyfriend. Russian. Gorgeous. Loves the hell out of you."

My lungs felt like someone had punctured them with nails. It hurt to breathe, and my head began to throb.

"Guess you guys broke up," Gwen said, more to herself than to me. "I hadn't heard. So you're engaged to…"

"Ori. Ori Abruzzo."

"Abruzzo," Gwen repeated and then shook her head.

"I don't think I've met him. How long have you been together?"

"I don't know," I whispered.

God, did I know *anything*?

I felt like such a fool, begging this Gwen person to fill in the blanks for me. I started to shake.

"Hey," she said, putting a hand to my shoulder again. "Take a deep breath. Good. Another one."

While I was sitting on the chaise, propped against the wall feeling like a marionette with all her strings cut, Ori came around the corner. "There you are. I was wondering what had—" He looked at Gwen.

"She wasn't feeling well, so I made her sit down," Gwen explained, rising. She held out her hand. "I'm Gwen James."

"Ori Abruzzo."

"Ah, the fiancé."

"How did—"

"Quinn and I are old friends." She looked at me for a moment. "Apparently she doesn't remember."

"She was in a car accident," Ori began.

"Yeah. She told me." She cocked her head to the side and studied Ori. "It was nice meeting you. Quinn, I hope you get your memory back soon. We should go out to lunch. The four of us. I'm sure Marshall would love to meet your fiancé."

Gwen's tone was biting, and I couldn't imagine why.

"I look forward to it," I said.

With one last look, Gwen strolled past Ori and disappeared. Ori came over and took a seat next to me. "You're really pale." He brushed the hair away from my cheek. "Jesus, you're cold too. Let's get you home."

He helped me up, wrapped an arm around me, and guided me toward the front. He dug in his pocket for our coat check number. The attendant found our coats and handed them over as Ori dropped a crisp bill into the tip jar.

This restaurant would no doubt remember us.

Ori helped me into my jacket and said, "Wait here while I have the car brought around."

I nodded and snuggled into my coat, pulling up the collar so I wouldn't get cold. Ori looped a gray cashmere scarf around his neck and buttoned his jacket as he stepped out into the dark night.

A few minutes later, Ori's car was brought around by the valet. Ori opened the passenger side of the car and waited for me to climb inside. It was brutally cold—the sky had been white all day, and the air smelled of snow.

When we had been driving for a few minutes, and the vents were blowing hot air onto my frozen toes, Ori asked, "What did she say to you?"

"Hmm?" I stared out the window, feeling the chill seep deep into my bones.

"Your friend. She said something to you. About your past."

I pinched the bridge of my nose. The headache was growing worse. No longer a dull throb but a constant blast of sharp pains.

Would the physical pain leave once my memory returned? Or was I now doomed to a life of headaches?

"Yes, Ori. She mentioned something about my past."

I glanced at him out of the corner of my eye. His jaw was clamped shut, and his hands gripped the steering wheel.

"She saw the ring," I said softly. "And she—she thought I was engaged to someone else."

"Who?"

"Sasha."

Saying his name was the equivalent of pulling a pin on an emotional grenade. I didn't dare say another word about him. About what else Gwen had said.

Loves the hell out of me.

If that had been the case, then why weren't we together? Had the loss of the baby driven us apart? Had we succumbed to our grief instead of clinging to each other?

I wanted to scream in frustration. Why? Why couldn't I know everything?

"Do you remember him?" Ori asked finally. His voice was soft, his placid tone attempting to lull me into confession.

"No. I don't remember him."

Ori let out a shaky breath.

I wanted to ask him if I had talked about Sasha, but asking my current fiancé to fill in the blanks about another man was cruel. To both of us.

I needed to talk to someone who knew. I needed to talk to Shannon.

And I couldn't get into my phone.

I had to get into my phone.

Lost in thought, I wasn't even aware that Ori had parked the car, and we were sitting in the driveway outside his house. Our house? I glanced down at the ring nestled on my finger.

I just needed a key. One key that would unlock the door to my memories. Unlock the door to everything I didn't know.

I unlatched my seatbelt and opened the door. Before I could protest that I was fine, Ori was there by the passenger side, grasping my hand and helping me out.

The sidewalk was slick with ice, and I slid into his body as we walked up to the house. Ori got out his keys and unlocked the door. I set my clutch on the foyer table and shrugged out of my coat. Ori took it from me and hung it up.

"I think the mood has been effectively ruined," Ori said dryly.

I forced out a laugh. "Yeah. I actually have a headache."

"Ah, Quinn, you don't need to use that old excuse."

"No, really," I said with a genuine smile. "My run-in with Gwen was exhausting."

Ori reached out and squeezed my shoulder. "Let's get comfortable, and I'll rub your head, see if we can do something about your headache."

He took my hand and led me up the stairs. Warmth curled through me when I remembered he was my fiancé, and he wanted to protect and take care of me. It made me wonder if I could take care of myself.

Chapter 13

QUINN

"Are you sure you're going to be okay for a few hours?" Ori asked, raking a hand through his dark hair.

I took a sip of coffee and forced myself to remain calm. "Yep. I'm just gonna hang out, watch TV, unpack all my clothes."

"I hate that I have to go into the office, but I've been ignoring stuff and—"

"I'll be fine, Ori." I smiled. "There's food in the fridge. I'll live until you come home."

He grinned. "How about takeout and a movie tonight?"

"Sounds good."

"And maybe we can try a repeat of last night? Before it all got derailed."

My heart skidded to a halt and then started drumming in my ears. Despite the murkiness of my unknown past, I still wanted Ori.

"I think that would be really…" I swallowed. "Nice."

"Nice?" He smiled. "Hopefully it will be better than nice."

Desire fluttered in my belly. Just like that, with a few simple words, I wanted him. I slowly unfolded my legs and got off the couch. I set my mug down on the coffee table and walked over to him.

My hands trailed up his chest. "We don't have to wait, you know. We could do it now. Before you leave."

"Do you really think our first time together since your accident is going to be a quickie?" His lips teased mine, and then his tongue was in my mouth. Before I knew it, I was holding onto him, gripping him tightly, begging him with my body.

"Quinn," he whispered as he tore his mouth from mine. He wrapped his arms around me and hauled me closer to him. I could feel him through his slacks, and I knew he wanted me as much as I wanted him. "It will be all right. We have all the time in the world."

We didn't, though. I felt something, an energy beneath my skin, a lurking knowledge just out of my reach.

Ori's fingers traced my cheekbones and then my jaw before pressing a light kiss to my lips. "I'll be home in a few hours." His words held a sensual promise I couldn't wait until he fulfilled.

Releasing me with a sigh, he then stepped away to grab his coat. With a wave, he was out the door. I stood there for a moment, waiting until I heard his car start and then the sound of the engine diminishing. When I was sure he was gone, and he wasn't going to come back for something he'd forgotten, I ran for his laptop computer in his home office. I didn't bother sitting in the office chair as I woke up the screen.

I cursed when I realized it was password protected. There would be no cyber stalking of myself. The only way to learn anything was to get into my phone. Yet, I still didn't remember the number password.

My eyes went to the landline telephone that rested on the desk. I picked it up, and soon I was asking the operator for the number of a cab company.

Twenty minutes later, I was in the back of a black town car, my cellphone gripped in my hand. When the car parked outside a cell phone store, I searched through my purse for some money and handed it over.

"Want me to wait?" the driver asked.

I shook my head. "I'm good. Thanks." I climbed out of the car and headed into the store. There were only two people in front of me, so I occupied my time by looking around at all the shiny gadgets.

"May I help you?" A young saleswoman monitoring the floor approached me.

I threw her a wide smile. "Yes, I'm hoping you can help me. I'm locked out of my phone, and I need to reset the password."

"Come with me," she said, gesturing to the corner of the store. She picked up a tablet and punched a few buttons. "Your phone number, please."

"Ah. I don't remember that."

The young saleswoman frowned. "I don't understand. How can you—"

"I'm suffering from short-term amnesia," I explained. "I can give you the name on the account, if that would help."

"Short-term amnesia, right." The woman looked me up and down. "I'm sorry, but I can't help you."

"Look," I said, trying to hold on to my patience. "I know this is weird, and you probably think I stole this phone, but I didn't. My name is Quinn O'Malley, and I'll show you my ID."

"I'm going to have to ask you to leave…"

With a grumble, I dug around in my purse and found

my license. I thrust it at her. "If I'd stolen this phone, do you really think I'd be that stupid as to come here? Look up the name on my account."

The woman's jaw clamped shut, and she turned off the tablet. "I'm getting a manager."

"Good," I stated.

Huffing, the woman whirled and stalked behind the counter. The manager leaned over, and the agent whispered in his ear. His eyes flew to mine and he nodded. A moment later, he came over with the tablet in hand. His smile was friendly but guarded.

"What can I help with you today, ma'am?"

"Hi," I said, smiling. Never hurt to turn on the charm, right? I quickly explained what I needed. I begged him to help me, even going as far as biting my lip and forcing tears. If he didn't help me, I was screwed.

"I'm very sorry, but we can't reset your password. If you can prove that's your phone, I can wipe it and restore it to its factory settings."

So I was shit out of luck until I remembered the password.

I sighed. "Okay. Thanks." I adjusted the purse strap on my shoulder and left. My plan had failed. I'd been hoping Shannon would call again and I could answer the phone, but it hadn't rung since last night. Ori was gone for a few hours. I thought about hitting a library to use a public computer and devour everything I could find on myself.

If only Shannon would just call me and then—

The universe finally heard my plea, and my phone rang. It was an unknown number, but I decided to answer it anyway. Anything to get me into the settings panel.

"Hello?" I answered.

There was silence on the other end of the line. Frowning, I looked at my screen. I was still connected.

"Hello?" I said again.

The line went dead. I looked at my phone—the screen was black. I pressed the home button and cursed. Locked out again. I wanted to throw the damn thing and watch it shatter.

"Excuse me!" someone called. I turned, and a gust of air hit me in the face. I gasped as I waited for the man to come to a halt in front of me.

"Hi," I said. "Do I know you?"

"I work at the phone store. I can tell you how to get into your phone."

Chapter 14
SASHA

The sound of her voice was a punch to my gut. It had been nearly a year since I'd heard it. But I'd never forget the timbre of it, the husky, raspy quality when I'd make love to her in the middle of the night.

God, the woman made me burn.

Was it too early for a drink?

I hadn't been back in the States for forty-eight hours, and I'd already called her. I knew it was only a matter a time before I went to Boston. I'd have to see her. I didn't care if she yelled, punched, clawed, or kicked me. I'd take it all. I'd take it all and win her back.

How the fuck did I win her back?

After breakfast, Campbell had left again, and Barrett had glued herself to my side. She'd refused to let me out of her sight. She called me a flight risk.

I came out of the bedroom to Barrett standing by the lit fireplace, a glass of scotch in her hand. Guess it wasn't too early for a drink after all.

"Fuck, I'm exhausted," I said.

Barrett didn't flinch at my vulgarity. The woman was

classy and elegant, and yet she'd gotten her hands bloody. Literally.

"Yeah, you look like hell," she remarked and took a sip of scotch.

"It's the burned face."

"That," she agreed. "I was also going to mention the massive bags under your eyes."

"You're a hell of a best friend, you know that?"

"Is it musty in here?" Barrett asked with a teasing grin.

"You know it's not." The girl who'd cleaned my apartment had done a thorough job. All the dust was gone. Everything gleamed. There were no remaining fragments of broken glass to be found.

It was like Quinn had never lived here.

"Guess we're starting the festivities early, eh?" I asked, nodding with my chin at her drink. It was just past noon and normal society dictated that it was bad to have a drink before the sun set. Luckily, Barrett and I had always seemed to play by our own rules.

"Did she answer?" Barrett asked as she went over to the liquor cart. She set down her glass of scotch so she could pour me a glass of vodka.

"I called Dimitri."

She handed me the glass and grinned. "Don't try lying to me. I can read you, you know."

I wondered if it was worth lying to Barrett. Then again, what did I really have to lose? I'd already lost Quinn—given her up and our life together.

Did I really have the right to show up again and blow her life apart?

"You talk to her…don't you?" I asked Barrett. I took a sip of the high-end vodka, letting it coat my tongue a moment before swallowing.

Barrett walked over to the white couch and sat down.

She ran her hand across the cushion. "I'd kill for a white couch. But with three boys who like to draw on furniture—and each other—white is a nightmare to clean. We've redecorated the castle. Gray hides everything."

I sighed. "You talk to her."

"Yeah, I talk to her." She slung back the scotch and then set her glass aside. "I can't believe I did that."

"Four hundred dollars a pour? You're supposed to savor it."

"We're about to talk about Quinn. I need some liquid courage."

"What do you know?"

She gestured with her chin to the vacant chair. I raised an eyebrow and then reluctantly sat down. "We didn't really speak this past year. I…tried. I called. Flynn called. Ash called. Duncan called. Brandon called—"

"Tell me she didn't fall in love with Brandon Kilmartin," I stated. "I don't think I can take hearing that."

Barrett shook her head. "No, Brandon and Quinn have never gotten together. As far as I know." She shook her head. "What are the chances that Flynn's cousin is a long-time family friend of the O'Malleys?"

"Yeah, I'm dying from the coincidence. Get on with it," I growled.

"She wouldn't talk to me because she thinks I chose you."

I frowned. "What do you mean?"

"Flynn and I didn't tell her you went to Russia. We kept that from her."

"You could've told her."

"I figured if you'd wanted her to know, you'd have told her yourself. So we kept it from her—until recently. Ergo, she thought we chose you and she got pissed. We reconnected recently… We went to Boston to pay our respects to her father."

"Death. Always bringing people closer together." My tone was dry, sardonic.

Barrett nearly snickered. "I had to break into her house."

"You broke into her house?" I let out a startled laugh. "Do you still make Campbell change the security code at the castle to give you a chance to practice?"

"Damn straight." She grinned. "I'm wondering how long I have to wait before I can teach Hawk."

"You do realize he's smarter than all of us, right?"

"God damn genius," she agreed, her smile bright when she mentioned her eldest son. "Anyway. I broke into Quinn's house. We got drunk. Made amends." She paused and folded her hands in her lap.

"What? What are you afraid to tell me?"

"I think she started dating someone, Sasha."

The air left my lungs, and suddenly I was cold. Colder than I'd ever been. And I'd weathered a few Russian winters without a coat when I'd been a child. Hearing that Quinn was dating was worse than all those winters combined.

"Who is he?"

She shook her head. "Don't know."

"You sure then?"

"She called me in the middle of the night. She talked in circles, and she didn't give any particulars. She sounded…scared. Of opening herself up again, but also determined, ya know? Like she couldn't bear the idea of living her life alone, yet she couldn't bear the thought of loving again either."

Guilt swamped me. I was so ashamed. But ashamed enough to let her go completely? That I didn't know.

I swallowed the nausea, forced it down and plowed forward. "Have you talked to her since?"

Barrett shook her head. "I've called a few times, left some messages. She hasn't called me back."

"You worried?"

"No. I think she's in a new relationship, Sasha. Where it's all…" She stopped suddenly and then reached for her empty glass. "Damn it." She got up and went to refill it.

"Where she's having sex nonstop with someone new," I finished for her, my tone bitter. "Bring me the bottle of vodka, Barrett. I need it."

Chapter 15

QUINN

I was home on the couch when Ori walked through the front door. A blanket was draped across my lap and the fireplace was blazing. "Hi," I called to him, shutting off the TV.

He came into the living room, still wearing his coat, and grinned. "You look cozy."

Throwing the blanket off, I got up and went to him. "It was a perfect day alone."

"That's not what you're supposed to say," he growled. "You're supposed to say, I love you, honey. I missed you, honey."

Grinning, I wrapped my arms around his neck. "I love you, honey. I missed you, honey. Take me to bed, honey."

Ori's eyes darkened. "You sure?"

"Yes."

"Do you want to talk about it?"

"We did just talk about it."

Ori swooped me up into his arms and headed for the stairs. I didn't think about anything except that I was going to see his body, watch it move over mine, come from mindless pleasure. I couldn't wait for it. I couldn't wait for him to see me.

I reached up and gently traced his jaw. It nearly made him stumble, but he righted himself. He looked down at me with a tender look in his eyes.

And suddenly, I wasn't nervous. Maybe I should've been, but this was Ori. He held the memories of our relationship so I didn't have to. One day, I'd remember them. Or I wouldn't. Either way, I wanted to spend my time, my life, with this man.

When we got to the bedroom, Ori set me down. I flopped onto the bed and grinned up at him. He smiled back and then climbed over me, settling his body against mine. Our lips meshed and greeted; it was like coming home. I'd made a choice and I'd chosen Ori. I'd chosen this moment and all the moments that came after. Maybe the ones before didn't matter. Maybe the past was just a shackle, binding me to pain and grief.

Love, planning for a future, new dreams…were so much better.

His fingers twisted in my hair as he angled my head. His mouth grazed my jaw and then my neck. And then his hands drifted down my body, eliciting chills and shivers of desire.

"Ori," I whispered.

"I know, Quinn. I know." His voice was raspy, like it caused him pain to go slow.

I didn't need slow. So I pushed against his chest, making him back up just enough so that I could shed my clothes.

His hands returned to my skin, teasing the curves of my breasts and belly. Lips traced the stretch marks. He loved them with his mouth, and then he scooted lower.

Parting my legs, he stared at the heat of me. His eyes darkened with desire, and he licked his lips.

There was no embarrassment or shyness. I expected there to be some, on my end, but there was nothing but lust and craving and demands.

He lowered his head and soon his tongue was lapping at my most sensitive place. His grip on my thighs tightened, and I closed my eyes, losing myself to the sensation of his tongue at my core.

I bucked and moaned.

He was greedy and demanding.

We were both impatient.

I shattered around him, my hands grasping his hair, the dark strands silk through my fingertips.

When he lifted his head, his eyes looked even darker. He climbed up my body and kissed me. The taste of me was on my lips, in my mouth. It drove me wild.

Ori pulled away to remove his clothes. I tried to roll him onto his back so I could love his body like he'd loved mine, but he shook his head.

"Later. I can't wait anymore to be inside you."

I spread my legs again and welcomed him.

He slid into me with an aching slowness. I felt him grow and harden even more, and sparks of pleasure shot down my spine.

"Wrap your legs around me, Quinn," he commanded. "And open your eyes. I need to see you."

My eyes flipped open.

Ori began to move, slow, infinitely slow, and then soon he was spearing into me with ferocity, like a warrior in the throes of blood lust.

I clung to him, but still my eyes remained open. Even as I felt tears seeping down my cheeks, I kept them open. I let him see all of me.

His hand reached down in between us to pluck the last bit of pleasure from me.

I screamed his name. And then his face contorted, a mask of pleasure and joy. He collapsed on top of me and gathered me close.

"Quinn," he panted in the curve of my neck. "God, Quinn."

I wrapped my arms around his back and squeezed. I leaned my cheek against his shoulder and sighed.

"Are you crying?" he asked.

"I—yeah. I guess I'm crying."

"Why?"

I brushed my lips against his salty skin. He smelled of us. "You've heard that some women are overcome by extreme emotion during this time, haven't you?"

He leaned up so he could look down at me. "Is that what happened? My prowess made you cry?"

I laughed, but it was strangled since Ori was still resting on my chest. He got the hint and gently rolled off me. He didn't go far, and then he placed his hand on the curve of my hip.

"Sometimes, moments are so beautiful, you can't help but cry." I reached up and pushed the hair away from his face. "Know what I mean?"

His smile was soft. "Yeah, I know what you mean."

I wiped the rest of the tears away and then burrowed against him. "I went to the cell phone store today."

"What? How did—what?"

"I called a cab. I wanted to know if they could reset the password to my phone."

Ori paused. "Did they?"

"No. Said they couldn't. They also thought I'd stolen it. Then this guy ran out after me and told me how to get into my phone."

"So you got into your phone? Do you remember anything?"

"I said he told me how to get into my phone, not that I followed his directions."

"I don't know what you're saying, Quinn."

Pulling away so I could look at him, I kept my eyes trained on his face. "I was going to do it. Get into my phone. Look at my photos, call Shannon, demand answers, but I had this thought." I took a deep breath. "The things I know—about losing my dad, the baby…those are sad, tragic moments—and maybe I'd have gotten my memories back if I'd looked at photos, and I could've remembered you, remembered falling in love with you, but I realized what that would also cost me. My past and all the unhappiness you said I was just coming through. So why do I have to remember, Ori? Do I have to remember?"

"Only if you want to. Only if you're ready."

His breath teased my cheeks, and I closed my eyes, wanting to savor the feeling of being completely bare before him. Not just in skin, either.

"Can't we build a life on what we have now? On new moments, on new dreams? If I remember, I remember, but for now…can't we just be? You and me—without all that stuff?"

Ori smiled and then leaned over to kiss me. "We can do whatever you want, Quinn. Let's make some new memories."

Happiness soared through me. I felt reborn and excited, excited for all the new things we could experience together.

He took my hand and laced his fingers through mine. "Speaking of new memories… Do you want to go to Italy?"

Chapter 16
SASHA

"How drunk am I?" Barrett slurred, her body slung across the couch, her legs up on the back of it.

"Pretty fucking drunk," I answered.

The fire was blazing, night had fallen, and a snowstorm was looming. We were safely ensconced in my apartment. There had been no word from Campbell all afternoon, but Barrett wasn't the type of wife to send him a bunch of text messages. She trusted him, he trusted her.

Then again, it would be interesting to see what Campbell would do when he realized I'd let his wife drink herself into a stupor. But no one ever told Barrett what she could or couldn't do. And I had no problem admitting to Campbell I thought his wife was the one who called all the shots. But I had a healthy dose of self-preservation, and Campbell had a strong right hook.

"Am I upside down?" Barrett asked.

"Just about."

"Why aren't you drunk?"

"I am drunk. I'm Russian. My drunk is melancholy and brooding."

She snorted. "Truth. Wow. My kids keep me in line. I can't drink like I used to."

I grinned. "What? Don't you and Ash leave your children with your husbands and then go out for a night of clubbing?"

"My best friend is now in bed by nine thirty every night and up at dawn. And clubs in Dornoch? You're kidding right?"

"Do you miss it?"

"Miss what?"

"Your life before children."

"Sometimes," she admitted.

"That was fast."

"What?"

"Your response. Do you regret them?"

"I didn't say that." She flung her legs off the back of the couch and swung around to sit upright. "Wow, no more scotch for me." Barrett put a hand to her head. "I just mean, kids are hard. You don't think about yourself first anymore. You can't. And you worry. All the time. I worry about them all the time, and I never forget about them. It's exhausting. But exhilarating."

"You didn't even want them," I said.

She smiled. "No, I didn't. But things change, and you meet someone who…who just becomes your everything, and you want half of you to mix with half of them and… and now I sound like I'm baking."

I laughed. "Yeah, you do."

"It's so good, though, Sasha." She shook her head. "There's this moment. Every morning. Flynn's still asleep, but I've just woken up, and the boys come into our room and jump on the bed. And we have this time where we're all laughing and tickling and wrestling before the day starts, ya know? It's the worst part about being away from home." She looked at me. "So no. I don't regret anything."

I leaned my head back against the chair. "I didn't care about kids. Not before her," I admitted. "I would've been fine if it had just been the two of us. But since she wanted them…"

"Really? That surprises me. You would've gone through with it just because she wanted them?"

I smiled. "It would've made her happy. So, yeah, I would've done it. It was the one thing we didn't really fight about, actually."

She snorted. "What did you fight about?"

"Everything. Nothing. Quinn is…passionate."

"She is that."

"In the beginning of our relationship, our fights always seemed to be about you."

"Yeah," she sighed. "I know."

"Quinn always said she wasn't an insecure, jealous person, but that my relationship with you brought it out."

"Flynn said the same thing. That changed over time."

I nodded. "Quinn mellowed, too."

"Well, she and I became friends—real friends. That helped."

"And then there was the accident, and I almost died, and then I didn't. We didn't talk about much that year I was bedridden."

She shook her head, and her hand went to her right hip. I didn't even think she was aware of it. She'd been in bed for the better part of a year too. God, how much we both had suffered, our bodies broken. Unsure if we'd ever feel whole again.

"You don't talk about things…when you're in a bed. You think about them, though. There were so many moments when all I wanted to do was scream and cry.

Throw things. But I couldn't. The boys didn't need to see me that way, see their mother broken in body—and spirit."

"What about Campbell?" I asked. I didn't have a pulse on how Barrett had weathered the storm because I'd been in the middle of my own.

"Flynn," she said slowly. "I kept it from him, too."

"How?" Guilt coursed through me. I'd been terrible—a bitter, angry monster that had lashed out at Quinn. The woman withstood it with quiet dignity, and she'd never wavered. No. I'd been the one to waver. I'd been the one to break over and over again.

"I wrote it all down." Her hand reached down to the knee that had never healed completely. Her right hip and knee had been shattered in a fall, but Barrett had somehow learned to live with it. Adapted. She was nothing if not adaptable.

"I filled so many journals, Sasha." She threw me a smile. "I thought about burning them. Symbolism and all that, but I realized that one day, I want the boys to read them. I want them to know me…when they're old enough."

"How do you protect them?" I asked. "When we live with the constant danger the way we do?"

"How do any parents protect their children?" she said with a shrug. "You make a choice. And you hold fast to it. Plus, they're guarded all the time."

"Valid point, Barrett."

I'd never wanted kids. Not after the childhood I'd had. The only good thing about being burned on the entirety of my right side was the fact that there were no longer physical reminders of my father on my skin. He'd used me as a human ashtray when I was seven years old. If there was any justice in the world, the bastard was rotting in hell.

"Oh, yay!" Barrett said, looking at her phone. "Flynn's

done with his meetings! Which means I get to have dinner with him. I should have dinner. I need something hearty to soak up all the peat in my stomach." She flopped back down onto the couch and smiled at me.

"Do you need my driver to take you back to The Rex?"

"Nope. Flynn is coming to get me. Should be here in about twenty." Her eyes drifted shut. "In the meantime, I'm gonna have a quick nap…"

Chapter 17

SASHA

"Where's my wife?" Campbell asked the moment I opened the door.

I grinned. "Passed out on the couch. She tried to drink me under the table."

Campbell strolled into the apartment and looked at his prostrate wife. "Clearly she failed."

"The only one who can outdrink me is you," I said with a clap to his back.

"It would be a shame to wake her." Campbell grinned at me. "Let me guess. She got into the scotch?"

"*Da*. We started early this afternoon."

"Of course you did." He said it without heat, and I knew he found it amusing that his average-sized wife tried to drink like a six-foot-five linebacker.

Campbell helped himself to a glass of scotch and then took a seat at the end of the couch. He looked at his wife and then grabbed the blanket off the back of the couch and covered her with it. It was thoughtful concern, and she always did the same thing for him. Got him glasses of water, rubbed his shoulders without a thought. They revolved around each other like two planets in orbit. Neither was the sun or the moon.

I retook my spot in the chair and looked out the window. The snow had started to fall, and I sighed.

"Going to Boston tomorrow?" he asked knowingly.

I nodded. "Not sure I should, though. But not sure if I can stay away."

"Don't make the choice for her," Campbell said, his cobalt blue eyes looking at the amber liquid in his glass. "You made the choice for her once when you walked away."

"No one will let me forget that."

"Do you? Let yourself forget it?"

My mouth quirked up. "Noted."

Campbell took a sip of his drink and then leaned back against the couch. "What are you going to do when you finally face her?"

"Plead? Beg? I don't know."

"So you don't have some grand plan to get her back? You're just going to show up on her doorstep and hope she doesn't slam the door in your face?"

"Knowing Quinn, she'll punch me in the jaw and *then* slam the door in my face."

"Sounds about right." Campbell looked thoughtful and cast a glance at his sleeping wife. "I'm worried about Archer's retirement."

"It really fucks up the entire thing we have going when he retires."

"That's the problem with a corrupt organization—you don't know who can be bought." Campbell flashed a sardonic grin. "I've got Archer putting out discreet feelers for anyone that can take his place."

I started to laugh. "You know what's fucking funny? There are those in this world who claim not to be criminals

—who do all this shit behind closed doors, but they're the ones more corrupt than us."

Campbell chuckled. The hand not holding his glass of scotch snuck underneath the blanket to rub Barrett's ankle. "Seriously. For once, it would be nice not to feel like I have to constantly put out fires. Sorry, bad choice of words." He grimaced. "What was it like? Walking away?"

I looked down and stared into my glass of vodka. "Honestly? I'm not sure. At times, I felt…relief. Like I didn't have to worry about anyone or anything. It was just me. Other times, I felt guilty."

"And you came back because…"

I sighed. "Unresolved issues."

"Crippling self-loathing, you mean?"

"You're an ass."

"I'm Scottish."

"Fine, you're an *arse.*"

Campbell grinned, but then it slipped. "Be damn sure, Sasha. If you're back, be back. But if you think for one second that you might need to walk away again, then you owe it to Quinn to leave her alone. You owe her the chance to be happy."

"Barrett said she thinks Quinn is dating someone."

"And that makes you feel…"

"Like I want to kill someone. Like actually walk down a dark alley and find some shithead and kill him."

Campbell sighed. "Welcome back, brother." He raised his glass to me and then took a sip.

Barrett stirred and then her eyes opened. "Hey. When did you get here?"

"Little while ago."

"Oh." She smiled sleepily. "Okay." Her eyes closed again, and her breathing evened out.

"We're flying home tomorrow," Campbell said. "We were supposed to fly out today."

"And you stayed because of me?"

Campbell shrugged. "There's always business I can do here. Besides, she needed this time with you."

I rubbed my jaw. It was sore from where Barrett had clocked me earlier. It wasn't even half of what I deserved. "Why didn't you hit me?"

"Because I wasn't pissed that you were gone."

"Ah, I knew it. You still actually hate me all these years later."

He shook his head. "Not even a little bit. I understood, Sasha. I understood why you needed to go. Just like I understand why you needed to come back. We should talk about backlash."

"What kind of backlash?"

"The Italians—or what's left of them—will hear that you're back."

"Fucking Italians," I muttered.

"It's not like it used to be. We don't kill off entire family lines. We don't murder women and children. We don't murder the innocent. We took their territory, but those neighborhoods remember. And there's always someone waiting in the wings to take over. Just be on your guard," Campbell warned.

"Dimitri hasn't said anything to me."

"There wasn't anything to say," Campbell said, finishing off his drink. "But I have a feeling we haven't seen the last of the Italians. It never ends when you think it ends. It never ends *how* you think it ends."

I sighed, suddenly feeling exhausted. "Does it ever end?"

Campbell smiled, but it wasn't in humor. "Aye. It ends. When one of us dies."

Chapter 18
SASHA

Boston weather sucked. It was worse than New York—if that was possible. It wasn't just cold, but brutal. And wet. So fucking wet you felt like you were walking around with frigid ocean water in your chest.

I grew up in Russia. I knew cold.

But I was in familiar territory. I'd spent a lot of time in this city. Before I'd even met Quinn, I'd come to Boston to do business with her father. I'd learned neighborhoods and the back alleyways; I'd learned which bars to go to for information. I'd learned how to be a shadow.

When half your face was scarred, you didn't have the ability of blending in anymore. I hardly noticed those who gaped when they saw me. That, too, didn't matter except for the fact that it made me memorable.

Dimitri had told me that when Quinn had left New York, she'd gone home to Boston. So I had my driver take me to her childhood home. He parked halfway down the block and put the car into idle.

When I made no move to get out, Sergei prompted, "Sir?"

"Right." I sighed and then reached for the door. I got out and then buttoned my coat. A blast of cold air hit me in the face, and I gritted my teeth as I walked toward the home Quinn had grown up in.

It was large and impressive yet still had the natural integrity of the surrounding neighborhood. It wasn't an eyesore. Though Michael O'Malley had been wealthy, he'd never been gaudy.

I'd debated on calling Quinn but quickly dismissed it. If she knew I was coming, she might not see me. I thought there was a better chance if I showed up unannounced. With a deep breath, I climbed the stairs to the front porch and then knocked on the door.

A moment later, it opened to reveal Michael O'Malley's young widow. She blinked in confusion, but it quickly cleared when she saw beneath the burned skin.

"You!" she spat.

I held up my hands in supplication. "Please. I need to see Quinn."

Jessica sneered. It was an ugly expression on a beautiful face. "She's not here."

"Do you know when she'll be back?"

"She doesn't *live* here anymore. She moved out."

I frowned. Her moving out must've been very recent because Dimitri had told me Quinn was still at her father's house. "Where does she live?"

"Like I'd tell you."

The woman was driving me insane, but I forced myself to rein in my temper. Losing it now would only cause Jessica to clam up further. "Listen, I can find out the information myself, but I'd rather just get it straight from you."

"What are you going to do? Hurt me?" she taunted.

I didn't know Jessica well at all. I'd only interacted with her at random social events, but that was the extent. There was no love lost between Quinn and her stepmother who was only a few years older than her. I was surprised by Jessica's surge of protectiveness.

This had been a bad idea. Jessica would probably call Quinn to give her a heads up I was in town and looking for her. I now fully expected Quinn to avoid the hell out of me—and I didn't want to waste any time tracking her down.

I turned away from Jessica and headed back to the car. I heard the slam of the front door but knew she was still watching me from the window. As I strode away, I reached into my pocket and pulled out my cell phone.

A moment later, I said, "It's Sasha."

Quinn's best friend was petite, blonde, and at the moment, shooting lasers at me with her eyes. Her husband stood behind her, also looking fierce—but he'd once played for the Patriots. But if there was anyone to be worried about, it was Shannon. She loved Quinn like a sister, and she was currently looking at me like I was nothing more than a diseased sewer rat.

"I hate your face," Shannon stated.

I nodded but said nothing.

Patrick leaned over and whispered something in his wife's ear. Reluctantly, she nodded and then stood back, allowing me entrance into her home.

I stepped inside. I'd been there a handful of times. We'd had many meals there. Broken bread together. I liked them both, not just because they were Quinn's best friends, but also because they were actually good people.

Protective. Loyal.

And I'd betrayed them by leaving Quinn.

"Take your coat?" Patrick said, holding his hands up.

Guess I'd be staying. A root canal would've been more fun, judging by the look on Shannon's face. She was about to put me through an inquisition, but I'd do anything if it meant finding out where Quinn lived.

And these people knew her. Maybe not all the parts of her. I knew they didn't understand why Quinn loved me.

Had loved me.

How she could've fallen for a criminal. But when that had been your entire life, even if you weren't a criminal yourself but had lived around them and flirted with the gray sides of the law, a normal person wouldn't understand.

"Would you like something to drink?" Shannon asked, politeness taking over the hostility. Only barely, though.

I shook my head. "No. Thank you."

The three of us stood awkwardly by the front door. It was Patrick who finally said, "Let's sit down." He guided his wife to the couch. She plopped down and watched me as I took my own seat in the chair.

"I wished I believed in violence, because I seriously want to do you bodily harm," she said.

Let the games begin.

Chapter 19
SASHA

My first instinct was to tell her to go to hell, to tell her that I wasn't accountable to her, and that the only person who I owed any sort of explanation to was Quinn. But Shannon was the first line of defense, and I had no chance of getting to Quinn without Shannon's help. More importantly, how I chose to handle this situation would determine if Shannon called Quinn to speak in my favor.

I needed all the favors I could get.

"If you want your pound of flesh, have at it," I said, tone mild.

Shannon's lips twitched, almost like she wanted to smile, but she locked that shit down. She glared at me instead. "Why should I tell you anything about Quinn?"

"You shouldn't," I said.

My answer clearly surprised her, and she unbent just a bit. "Well, you've got me on the hook. Don't stop now."

"I hurt her. I know that. I don't deserve a second chance, but I'm willing to fight for it anyway." I swallowed. "Barrett told me she's dating someone?"

"You spoke to Barrett?" Shannon's blue eyes, which

had been soft moments ago, were now narrowed into slits of rage. "The first thing you do when you come back is to talk to *that woman.*"

"Don't," I said, my tone gentle but not lacking in force. "You don't get to flay me alive because I sought out my best friend."

"Best friend. Right," Shannon muttered.

"I'll explain anything you want me to explain. Why I left, why I had to do it, why it cost me everything. I needed to be right in my own head, and I didn't know if I'd ever be able to get it all sorted. I'll explain all that. I'll even write shitty poetry and show it to you if you think it will help me win Quinn back. But under no circumstances will I explain to you anything about my relationship with Barrett."

"I don't need your explanation, Sasha. I've heard it from Quinn plenty of times."

"Barrett and Quinn are friends, you know?"

Shannon shrugged. "I've known Quinn since we were kids."

"Oh, I get it." I smiled. "You're jealous."

"I'm not jealous."

Patrick placed a hand on his wife's shoulder. "Easy."

She reached up and took his hand and then let it go. "I'm not jealous," she said again, her tone softening.

"What's that saying? If it walks like a duck?"

Shannon's cheeks bloomed with color. "What do I have to be jealous about?"

I leaned back in the chair and decided to douse the fire with gasoline. "Does Quinn call *you* in the middle of the night when she has questions about life? No? Didn't think so. She calls Barrett. Because Barrett understands Quinn on a level that you never will."

"Because I'm not involved in organized crime? Spare me that explanation."

I knew I'd gotten under her skin. I wasn't proud of it. Or maybe I was. "I like you, Shannon. I've always liked you. And Quinn considers you family. She calls Barrett because"—I paused— "because Barrett has done the worst things a person can do, and Quinn doesn't feel like…like she's being judged."

"I don't judge her." Her face slackened when she thought of the possibility her best friend in the entire world was concerned about her opinions. "I just worry about her. All the time. She holds it all in, you know? You…got hurt. She kept it in. You left…she kept it in. The only time she didn't keep it in was when she lost the baby."

My breathing stilled. "Baby?"

"The baby," Shannon repeated, a frown marring her face. She stared at me, her eyes darting back and forth. "Oh my God. You didn't know."

"Quinn was pregnant?" My voice came out raspy, gritty.

Quinn. My Quinn. Pregnant. Alone.

It felt like I'd run across a mountain, through valleys and canyons. I was winded and exhausted. And confused. So fucking confused. "What—what happened?"

"You left," Shannon said quietly. "She came back to Boston. She found out a few weeks later. She was twenty weeks along, Sasha, when she lost it. *Him.*"

"A boy?" I whispered, feeling the blood drain from my face. "How did she—why did—"

"She fell down the stairs," Shannon said, tears finally starting to seep out of the corners of her eyes to dribble down her fair cheeks. "And as soon as she was coming out of that, her dad got diagnosed."

I placed my head in my hands. Bleak torment engulfed

me. Just when I thought I'd be able to deal with the guilt of leaving Quinn so I could handle my own demons, she'd needed me. Needed me the most and I'd abandoned her.

"I didn't know," I said, looking up. "I swear to God, I didn't know."

"Barrett…she didn't tell you?"

I shook my head. "I don't think she knew. Otherwise…"

"Otherwise she would've told you," Shannon accused.

"*Da*. Barrett and I don't keep secrets from one another."

"Which is why Quinn didn't tell her," Shannon guessed. "It feels disloyal. Telling you about the baby."

"I know."

Patrick still hadn't said anything, but he didn't seem inclined to. He just stood behind the couch, his hands resting on Shannon's shoulders. His eyes were somber when he looked at me.

Pity.

Fuck all the pity.

Shannon inhaled a shaky breath. "Do you want to see where your son is buried?"

Chapter 20
SASHA

I stood in front of a modest gray headstone engraved with the month and year. And his name.

Shannon and Patrick were waiting in the car. They'd offered to stand with me, but I wanted time alone. Time to grieve for the life I'd walked away from, time to grieve for the son I'd never know. Now, more than ever, I had to talk to Quinn. I wanted to hear the story from her lips. I wanted to take her pain, kiss away the tears, cry for the past, and broach a new future.

I said some words in Russian as my gloved hand reached out to touch the grave marker.

What had she looked like, round with my child? Had she been nervous? Serene? Had she rejoiced or cursed?

It was killing me not to know.

A wave of anger swept through me. I curled my hand into a fist. She'd kept this from me, purposefully and with cause. To hurt me?

God, I had so many questions and none of the answers.

I'd find her and demand them.

With one final look at the headstone, I memorized it, and then turned away. As I walked back toward the car, I was assaulted by a memory of a time when we'd been happy. When everything had been new and there was nothing but the promise of a life together. When I'd been whole. When I'd look in the mirror and recognize the man who stared back. When I'd look in the mirror and not grimace at the gruesome sight.

"I've always liked the name Rupert," Quinn said.

"You're certifiable if you think I'd ever name our son Rupert.*" I looked at her and brushed the hair away from her cheek.*

She laughed. "Gotchya! I'd never saddle a kid with that name. Something Russian, perhaps?"

"I'd rather name him Rupert."

Quinn snuggled against me and pressed her lips to my naked chest. "I guess we're jumping the gun talking about baby names when there isn't even a baby."

I rolled her onto her back and pushed her deeper into the mattress. Grinning wickedly, I lowered my head. "So let's make one."

I opened the car door as the memory cleared. Every breath I inhaled hurt. Like I'd swallowed glass, and with each pulse of my heart, the shards embedded deeper, cut me faster. If I bled out, it would be a blessing.

Patrick was in the driver's seat and looked at me in the rearview mirror. Shannon turned around. Her face was pale, and her eyes were red-rimmed.

"Get what you needed?" Shannon asked.

I let out a strangled laugh. "Hardly."

She reached out, and I immediately took her hand. It was small, childlike, the bones delicate like a bird. I could crush her. Instead, I brought her fingers to my lips. With a squeeze, I let her go.

"What will you do when you see her?" Shannon wondered.

Laugh. Cry. Yell. Pull her close and never let her go again.

"I guess that depends on Quinn."

"You're going to give her a choice?" Patrick asked in surprise, finally speaking. He'd been quiet this entire time, letting Shannon dictate the conversation. "Like you gave her a choice when you walked away?"

"Like she made a choice by not telling me about the baby," I threw back.

We all fell silent again as Patrick drove away from the cemetery. The bare trees were gray and white blurs through the glass. I felt lost and alone, abandoned to my own emotions coursing through me. All I wanted to do was check into my thousand-dollar-a-night penthouse hotel suite and drink myself into a stupor. Productive? No. But I was Russian and good at brooding.

"Where are you staying?" Shannon asked when Patrick turned the corner.

I gave her the name of the hotel and then leaned my head back against the seat. "You still haven't told me where Quinn is."

"I still haven't told you a lot of things," Shannon muttered.

"What does that mean?" I demanded.

Shannon glanced at Patrick.

"Tell him when we get to the hotel," Patrick said.

An ominous feeling overtook me. I curled my hands into fists again. Before I drank away the night, I needed to spar. I needed to feel my muscles burn, my body ache. Only then would the alcohol help me sleep. As it stood, I needed a fight or a fuck.

And I hadn't fucked since Quinn.

Hadn't made love since her either.

Patrick pulled up in front of the hotel and put the car

into idle. Then he nodded at his wife. She turned around to look at me, holding the words in her mouth, more words that had the power to destroy me.

"She was in a car accident a few days ago. She's fine," she rushed to add. "Physically."

My heart leapt into my throat. "Physically?"

"Quinn hit her head in the accident. And she…she has amnesia."

Booming laughter shot out of my mouth and resounded in the car. "You're fucking kidding me."

"I wish I was. I haven't been able to see her. According to her *boyfriend*"—she paused— "the doctor gave strict instructions that she wasn't to be told anything about her past. She needs to learn about everything in her own time."

"That's the fucking stupidest thing I've ever heard."

Quinn had amnesia. Which meant she probably didn't remember me. Maybe that was a blessing. *Screw that.* She needed to remember me. Remember us. It was the only way I could win her back.

"So you're telling me, that on top of asking for a second chance, I have to make a woman who doesn't remember me, fall in love with me all over again?"

"Don't men love challenges?" Shannon asked with a tremulous smile. "I'm sorry, Sasha."

"Why haven't you seen her?" I demanded. "You're her best friend. If anyone had a chance of jarring her memory, it would be you."

"Ori said she was in a very fragile state and that it would be better to wait. He gave me the name of Quinn's doctor, and he confirmed that it was better to wait for me to see her."

"Ori?" I asked slowly.

"Ori Abruzzo," she clarified. "The boyfriend."

"Have you met him?"

She shook her head. "Quinn was about to introduce us when she had the accident. I've never met him. But she…"

"Go on," I growled.

"Hey," Patrick voiced. "Don't take that tone with my wife."

I raised an eyebrow. There were alpha males, and then there were mafia alpha males. The two weren't even in the same ring. I only backed off out of respect.

"Sorry," I said. "Please continue."

Shannon flashed me a genuine grin, but then it faded. "She was just getting happy, Sasha. This Ori guy made her…sound like her old self."

"She has to remember me, Shannon. I need her to."

Blue eyes searched mine as she asked a silent question that I answered, "Because I can't be myself without her."

Chapter 21

SASHA

Sometimes there was nothing better than beating the shit out of a sandbag. It couldn't hit back. It just stood there, strong, steady, and took all my anger.

Thwack.

Thwack.

Thwack.

Panting, I stopped. I'd been going at it for an hour.

The amazing thing about having more money than you knew what to do with? You could call a hotel front desk and demand things. Things like installing a sandbag in the actual penthouse.

I missed my apartment in the Meatpacking District. It was decked out exactly how I wanted. I'd sparred with Barrett on the lower floor. I'd tried to teach Quinn a thing or two. All we'd ended up doing was having sex on gym mats.

God, that woman.

With renewed vigor, I attacked the sandbag again. When I was finally spent, I collapsed my sweaty body on the couch. I removed the tape from around my knuckles and flexed them.

I'd hurt in the morning. Good. I deserved to hurt.

Getting up, I groaned, already feeling my muscles cooling down. I reached for my phone on the glass coffee table. Dimitri answered on the first ring.

"I need information on Ori Abruzzo."

"*Da,*" Dimitri said in confirmation and then hung up.

That was the reason he was my second. He didn't ask questions, he didn't quibble, he just got shit done. It was why I'd left the Russian territory in his very capable hands. He'd not only held the territory, but he'd expanded it. Parts of Brooklyn and Queens that had been Greek or Polish, Dimitri had taken over. With minimal bloodshed.

I didn't seek out violence, but I doled it out when necessary.

Igor had made sure of that.

"Brother," I whispered.

I wondered if Igor's ghost could hear me.

Igor and I had both been untried men, soldiers in his father's *Bratva*. Young idealists who'd wanted a different life but knowing there was no way out. When Igor had taken over, and I became his second in command, he'd made me swear that if he put the brotherhood in jeopardy, if he deviated from trying to get us all a better life, that I'd put him down.

I had been his balance and check system, and now he was dead. Near the end, Igor hadn't been the man I knew. But that was a rationalization for what I had done, and now I was forever haunted by the ghost of a man who'd I'd considered a brother.

Sins demanded payment. But apparently, not enough had been taken from me. I'd lost an eye, the woman I loved, and our child.

When would the suffering end? Or would it. Maybe this was my path. Anger, hatred, scars, burns, blood, ashes.

Self-loathing and hatred consumed me. I shot up off the couch and grabbed the bottle of the highest-end vodka the hotel had in its bar. I unscrewed the lid and drank right from the bottle.

A mafia king who knew how to drink like a soldier.

None of it mattered. Not the power, not the money, not the ability to order a woman to her knees—they were always too willing, too eager.

Barrett hadn't been. She'd been a fighter, from the very beginning, but I'd seen how she manipulated Igor. I saw her for what she was—a woman in love with her husband but desperate to hold power in her own right. And she did.

Quinn hadn't been eager. Not in the beginning. When I'd approached her in the restaurant where she'd been eating with Shannon, she'd told me to go fuck myself. Her words had mirrored her actions. She'd dismissed me with a careless turn of her shoulder. She hadn't been a woman who said one thing and truly meant another.

I'd wanted her. From the beginning. She was a challenge, but when I won her, the reward would be far greater than the chase. Because Quinn was a woman you caught and never let go.

If Ori Abruzzo was smart, he'd recognize the same quality. If he was smart, he'd let her go or I'd kill him.

I dragged my exhausted body to the bathroom. After taking another swig of vodka, I set the bottle down onto the sink counter and started the shower. Steam billowed in clouds, and I closed my eyes. Stripping off my clothes, I refused to look in the mirror. I knew what I looked like. The right side of my body was shriveled and ugly. I'd almost wasted away, but I'd come back stronger. Not only in body, but in mind too.

Quinn would need me to be strong. I'd be strong enough for the both of us. And damn it, she'd remember me. She'd remember it all. She would yell and scream, cry and hit. She'd laugh and sigh, and then she'd let me hold her. She'd let me hold her, make love to her, and give her another baby because that's what I wanted more than anything in the world. At one time, Quinn and I had had the same dreams. It was time to remind her.

I washed quickly and shut off the shower. Droplets dribbled down my skin as I reached for a towel. I quickly dried my short blond hair—or what was left of it—and did the same to my body. I dropped the towel. Completely nude, I strode into the bedroom and stopped short.

A young woman with black hair was lying in the middle of my bed. Her breasts spilled out of her lacy black bra. Her matching lace panties were nothing more than a scrap of material hiding the most intimate part of her. She smiled bright red lips as her eyes hungrily raked over me.

"Hi." Her voice was husky. Pure seduction.

I said nothing.

She slid off the bed and sauntered toward me. She was petite but had curves. Her eyes skimmed over my face. Either she didn't care I was hideous, or she was being paid enough to pretend she wanted me.

Before she could wrap her arms around my neck, I took a step back. Her grin widened, clearly liking the challenge. I wasn't in the mood for bullshit.

"Get out."

She blinked, her bravado slipping for a moment; then her mask was back in place.

"You seem a little wound up. I could help with that." She reached out to touch me, but I was faster. Before she knew it, I had my hand around her throat and her body pushed up against a wall.

"Wound up?" I asked, pitching my voice low. "Not wound up. Just pissed as fuck that a random woman is in my hotel room. How did you get in here?"

With her eyes widening in fear and her hands clawing at mine which held her neck, she couldn't answer. I squeezed for a moment and then let go. She fell to the floor, coughing and gasping, black tracks of mascara cascading down her face.

"The concierge sent me." Her voice still sounded strangled.

"Did I ask for you?" I demanded.

She shook her head.

"You might want to tell them that I didn't have to stop squeezing."

She lifted her head, eyes shiny with more tears waiting to fall. Her lip trembled, but then she nodded again. She got up off the floor and scurried out of the room.

I would have never killed a woman just for showing up in my room, but she didn't need to know that. I was still a mafia king. It wouldn't hurt to remind people of it.

Chapter 22
SASHA

After I got dressed, I called down to the front desk and had a few words with the manager. When I hung up, I swore I could smell his fear even floors above him.

I'd be lying if I said I didn't get off on it a little bit.

Dimitri was doing his due diligence and finding out everything there was to know about Ori Abruzzo. Shannon had given me Quinn's new address, and tomorrow, I had plans to see her. It was a dangerous game, confronting her in the state she was in. But how could I not go to her? How could I not help her get her memories back?

I settled on the couch with the bottle of vodka. My cell phone rested on the cushion next to me. Even after all this time, Barrett was still the one I wanted to talk to first whenever there was something I had to work out in my mind. She was my confidante, and she was the person I talked to when I needed advice about Quinn. She'd always been that for me. Quinn and I had fought endlessly about it. She thought me confiding in Barrett meant I wasn't confiding in her. Maybe that had been true. Maybe I'd wanted to shield Quinn from the darkness inside of me. I'd never wanted that darkness to touch her.

"Yeah," Barrett said into the phone. No greeting, no acknowledgment.

"Bad time?" I took a sip from the bottle.

"No. Well, sort of. We walked through the door about twenty minutes ago. The bairns are climbing the walls."

"Literally?" I asked with a smile. I wouldn't put it past Barrett's kids. They were a unique breed of trouble.

She snorted. "Can you give me a few minutes to call you back? I'm trying to wrestle them into bed."

I paused.

Barrett sighed. "Oh, okay. Hold on."

A moment later, I heard her far-off call telling Campbell to handle their children and then Barrett was back. "I'm in the library. So talk away."

"Where do I even start?"

"The beginning?"

"Quinn was pregnant."

Silence reigned on the other end of the phone.

"When?"

"After I left her." I explained what I knew.

"Fuck," Barrett stated. "I didn't know, Sasha, I swear. Poor Quinn."

I suddenly understood why Quinn hadn't told Barrett. It hadn't been because of me. It had been because Quinn couldn't stand pity, and that's all Barrett would've been able to show her. Not to mention, she had three healthy beautiful children with Campbell—a man who'd never abandoned her.

Quinn had pride, and Barrett's sympathy would've cut her off at the knees.

"How are you feeling about all this?" she wondered.

"How am I feeling about finding out that Quinn was

pregnant and then losing the baby? Jesus, how do you think I feel about it?"

"How much of the vodka bottle have you drank?"

I held it up. "About a third."

"Less than I expected. I really don't know what to say. I wish she'd told me. I wish I could've been there for her."

"She didn't want you there. Shannon was there." A lump of emotion formed in my throat, when I thought of Quinn in the hospital—thin, pale, with wires coming out of her arm as Shannon sat with her.

"How'd you find out?" Barrett asked.

"Shannon." I sighed. "There's more."

"More? More than that? What else is there?"

"Quinn was in an accident a few days ago—apparently she has amnesia."

"You've got to be fucking kidding me!"

"So on top of all of this, trying to find her, trying to explain to her…everything… I now have to contend with a memory issue. What am I supposed to do, Barrett?"

"I don't know. Kidnap her? Force her to remember you?" she said. "Sorry, I'm really tired."

"It's late there. It's late here. Go to bed. We can talk tomorrow. I just wanted you to know. You can tell Campbell."

I gave her permission because sometimes Barrett and I didn't share each other's confidences with our significant others. We guarded each other's secrets. Apparently, this wasn't normal behavior, but then again, Barrett and I were hardly normal.

"You sure?"

"*Da*. Yes. I'm sure."

"You going to be okay?"

I held up the vodka bottle again. Light spilled through the clear liquid. "Yeah, I'll be fine."

"Sleep on your side so you don't choke on your own vomit."

"God, Campbell is a lucky devil. Tell him I said so."

"Love you," she said.

"Love you."

We hung up, and I tossed my phone aside. I looked at it, willing it to ring, but of course it remained silent.

So I did what any man in my position would do, I drank. I drank and I talked to the ghost of Igor Dolinsky who had a lot of wisdom on the subject matter of losing the woman you loved and the child she carried. That was the thing about vodka and sleep deprivation. Even though I knew I was talking to myself, I still imagined Igor's voice and I swore I could hear his laugh.

And for now, it was enough.

I awoke to the sun streaming through the gauzy curtains of the hotel window. Let it be known that a high-end vodka hangover in an expensive hotel suite was still a hangover. Would it have been worse if I'd woken up with my face against scratchy linens and a cheap air conditioning unit humming near my ear?

Yes.

But a hangover was a hangover.

Rolling over onto my back, I stared up at the ceiling and scratched my chest. The puckered skin on my right pectoral was a reminder of my imperfections.

If Quinn didn't remember me, all she would see in front of her was a badly scarred man. Would it terrify her? Would she force out her chin and meet my eyes?

I needed to know.

My cell had fallen between the couch cushions. When I fished it out, I saw I had no missed calls. I wanted to throw it in frustration, but even Dimitri needed time to find out information.

After a quick shower, I dressed and headed for the

lobby. I stopped off in the café/restaurant for breakfast and coffee. The day was cold but bright.

Sergei was waiting for me, and when I climbed into the car, I gave him Quinn's new address. My heart thundered inside my chest. I was about to come face to face with her.

What if she wasn't home? What if she was staying with Abruzzo?

I'd sit outside her apartment building until she came back.

The car pulled to a stop, and I immediately got out and stalked half a block to her apartment building. I frowned when I realized it was an old brownstone. Not at all Quinn's taste. Hadn't been anyway. Maybe she'd changed.

I'd certainly changed. It was stupid to think she hadn't.

I opened the door to the vestibule, only to realize that if Quinn was home, there was a good chance she wouldn't open the door for a stranger. I studied the lock on the door and smirked. Making short work of it, I was soon taking the stairs to the third floor. Quinn O'Malley, living on the third floor of a walk-up? The surprises just kept coming.

When I got to her door, I stopped. I'd lived through a fire, gunshots, and losing my best friend, and I'd rather live through all those things again than face the woman on the other side of the door. Which was why I forced myself to knock.

There was no answer.

I knocked again.

When it was clear she wasn't home, I let out a sigh. Part relief, part annoyance. And then I heard the sounds of footsteps on the stairs, and my heart kicked into high gear.

An older man rounded the corner of the stairwell. His bushy brows rose when he saw me. "Help you, sir?"

He wore a set of keys on his belt. The super.

I flashed a smile and held out my hand. "Hi."

The man looked at my hand and then took it. "Hello."

"I'm old friends with the woman who lives in this apartment," I said, gesturing to the door behind me. "I'm in town on business. Wanted to surprise her."

His eyes narrowed in suspicion. "How did you get in here? The building is old, but you have to be buzzed in."

"The door to the foyer didn't catch all the way. It was open."

The man unbent as he dropped my hand. "I need to take a look at that."

"Probably a good idea," I agreed. "So…the woman?"

He studied me for a moment, and then he finally said, "I'm afraid she moved out."

"Really? I got her address from her best friend just yesterday."

He nodded. "She moved in and then broke her lease a few days ago. Hadn't even lived here a month. Her boyfriend called, said she was in an accident and that she was moving in with him so he could take care of her. Nice fella."

I looked at the door. "Did she leave a forwarding address?"

"Nope. Sorry."

"Right," I muttered. "Thank you."

"Nice young woman," the man said. "Unfortunate about her accident."

"Yeah. It is." I moved past him and then headed down the stairs.

Another fucking roadblock.

As I went out into the cold, my phone rang. Adrenaline shot through my veins. Hopefully it was Dimitri.

"Shannon," I greeted, disappointment slithering through me.

"Hey," she said, her voice hesitant.

"What is it? Is it Quinn?"

"It's—yeah. It's Quinn. She's fine."

"Fine? Why don't I believe you?"

"I don't know how to say this, but okay. I'm just going to say it."

"Say what," I growled.

"Quinn is in Italy."

"Italy?"

"Yeah. They flew out yesterday."

"All right." I pinched the bridge of my nose. I got to the car and was just about to open the door, when Shannon's next words stopped me.

"Ori told me—Sasha, they're engaged."

It was like I'd fallen through the ice of a lake in winter. Jagged, piercing pain.

"How? How is that possible? She's got amnesia, for Christ's sake."

"I'm worried about her, Sasha. I think Ori—I think he might be coercing her—"

Cold calm rage took over. "I'll handle it."

"Good."

I hung up.

Time to go to Italy.

Chapter 24

QUINN

Ori took my hand and guided me toward the quaint white-washed stone villa in a tiny little town I'd never heard of. Or maybe I had heard of it once, but now with amnesia I'd forgotten. Instead of dwelling on that thought, I decided to focus on the here and now.

"You own this?"

He smiled. "It's been in my family for generations. Come look at this kitchen." We walked through the front door and passed the sitting room. It was warm and inviting, but Ori gave me no time to dwell on it. He tugged me along until we got to the kitchen.

"Oh," I breathed. The room had a long dining room table, large enough to seat twenty, but that wasn't what had caught my attention; it was the view out of the expansive windows. Rolling hills and in the distance, a vineyard. "You've got to be kidding."

Ori wrapped his arms around me from behind. "It's pretty good, right?" His lips brushed my ear and I shivered. "Some of the best wines from Abruzzo come from the vineyards in the hills of Teramo."

I closed my eyes and leaned against him, listening to him speak. At one point his English turned to Italian, and I was unable to resist it. Turning in his arms, I leaned up to kiss him.

His mouth captured mine, and then I felt myself being maneuvered backward. I thought he was leading me to a bedroom, but Ori surprised me when he lifted me in his arms and plopped me down on the countertop. He stepped forward, wedging my knees open.

I sighed into his mouth as his hand rested at the seam of my jeans. He pushed with the heel of his palm. I moaned. Before I knew it, Ori had my zipper down and my jeans unbuttoned.

"Lift up," he growled.

I rested my hands on the counter and then pushed up so Ori could pull my pants down. My panties went with them. Ori's eyes darkened as he spread me open. "Lie back," he commanded.

Shuddering from the delicious sensations, I obeyed.

His thumbs peeled back my folds, and then his tongue was on me. He showed no mercy as he devoured me, his strong tongue lapping at me like he couldn't get enough.

When I reached for him, he lifted his head and said, "Hands on the counter."

My fingers gripped the edges of the granite, and when Ori was satisfied, his tongue was back, and I was shivering with need.

But before Ori let me go over the edge, he pulled away again. Just long enough to stand and undo his belt. His pants hit the floor, and he took his hard length in his hand and pumped a few times. He came toward me again.

"I want to taste you," I whispered.

"Later," he answered, tone gruff. "I need to be inside you."

I glanced down at him. We were engaged, and we both wanted babies. I spread my legs. With a growl, Ori grasped my hip and eased himself inside of me.

It was the most amazing thing, Ori stretching me, his strokes long and hard. I whimpered when I felt him grow harder, spearing me, taking it all. His thrusts were relentless, branding me, owning me.

I wrapped myself around him and held on until he drove us to the brink of madness. But finally—finally—I came, tightening around him, holding him close.

With a guttural grunt, his release followed.

He drew me to him, his lips dropping to the curve of my neck to place a smattering of kisses along my skin. "I feel like my entire life led up to this moment," he admitted.

I nodded against him. "Yeah. I know what you mean."

"Are you okay? That we…"

"Yeah."

Ori leaned back so he could look me in the eyes. His hands reached up to cradle my cheeks, his thumbs sweeping across my lips. "The church my parents were married in is a twenty-minute drive from here." He stared into my eyes. "But I can't—I can't ask you to tie your life with mine when you don't remember your past."

His gaze was intense, unwavering. Waiting.

"Ori," I whispered. "I might not ever remember. We've been through this, haven't we?" I frowned. "I have this feeling, like the life I was living was so…unhappy. You told me I was just coming out of it, ya know? I want to stay here. In this moment. Forever."

"You don't want to remember?"

"Why would I want to remember? Remember all the grief, all the losses? The flashes of memories I've had—most were sad. I'm worried it's all sad."

"Nothing is all one thing or the other," he said, moving

ever so slightly. He was still inside of me, still hard, still needy.

I was needy too.

"Marry me, Ori," I whispered. "Marry me and let's be happy."

His hands dropped from my face to slide down my body. "You sure, Quinn?"

"I'm sure."

Ori began to move again, thrusting gently, rocking against me. "I'm going to make you so happy, Quinn," he whispered as his mouth took mine.

Chapter 25

QUINN

Our interlude on the kitchen counter hadn't been enough. He lit candles and then made love to me in his bed. Night had fallen.

I should've been suffering from jet lag. But what was jet lag when the man of your dreams was currently rubbing essential oils onto your skin and worshiping you with his hands?

We'd been naked for hours. It felt decadent and frivolous, yet I couldn't imagine doing anything else. Even though Ori had promised me the stars were brighter here than anywhere else, I had no desire to move to see them. Maybe tomorrow night.

"Tell me what you want," Ori said as his hands kneaded my back.

"Right now? Nothing."

"I mean, out of life."

"What did I want before?" I asked. "Before I lost my memory."

"No. That's not how this works."

I smiled into the pillow. "How does this work?"

"You tell me, right now, what you want out of life."

"I don't know, Ori. I have no idea what I'm good at. No idea if I had any hobbies."

"That's why I'm asking. You're a blank canvas, Quinn. You're practically a newborn. You get to do new things, try new things."

I closed my eyes and let his hands continue their journey across my body. "Right now, all I want to do is this. Be with you. Drink Italian wine, eat Italian cheese. Live, you know?"

Did I have a job? I didn't know. Did it matter? Did it bring me joy? Fulfillment? Satisfaction?

How did Quinn O'Malley spend her time before she'd lost her memory? Who was she? I had no idea and Ori wasn't inclined to tell me. A bubble of frustration welled up inside of me, but I popped it. No. Losing my memory had been a blessing.

My parents were gone.

I'd lost a child.

How much more sadness had I endured?

I knew enough, and I didn't want that life. I didn't want to go back to it.

"Quinn?"

"Hmm?"

"Why are you tense?"

I instantly relaxed. "Am I a coward for not wanting to remember?"

"No. You're not a coward."

"Shouldn't I want to, though? Remember my identity? Remember you?"

"What do you feel when you think of me?" he wondered.

I thought for a moment, and then I smiled. "Safe. You make me feel safe."

He paused and then, "Anything else?"

"Desire."

"What else?" he pressed.

"Loved. Cherished. Happy. I think I could be truly happy with you, Ori—without having to remember everything."

His hands stilled, and then he collapsed onto the bed next to me. He stared at me with deep brown eyes and said, "Whatever you want, I'll get it for you. You want to be a wife and a mother? I'll make it happen. You want to learn to paint, or make cheese, then I'll find the best people to instruct you."

I reached out to gently swipe his hair off his forehead. "Would *you* be happy, though? If I…I don't know, never found my purpose?"

"What is purpose anyway? Do you know how many people go to bullshit jobs to make a shitty living to support their unhappy, ungrateful families? I have more than enough money to take care of us. And there's nothing wrong if all you want is to be a wife and a mother and to have nice things. I'll take you around the world. I'll give you so many good memories that even if you remember the bad ones, it won't matter."

I smiled. "I already said I'd marry you. Why are you trying so hard?"

"I don't just want to marry you. I want to take care of you. Will you let me be good to you, Quinn?"

I snuggled into his embrace and let out a sigh. "Do we have to live in Boston? I mean, do you have to be in Boston for your work? What do you do, anyway?"

He snorted. "A little of this a little of that."

"That doesn't tell me anything," I teased.

Ori laughed. "Does it matter what I do? It pays for first-class flights to Italy."

I moaned, remembering the reclining seats and never-ending mimosas. "You do know how to treat a girl. You remembered to call Shannon, didn't you?"

He nodded. "I did."

I rolled over onto my back to stare at the ceiling. "Most people would've called their best friend to share the news."

"Most people remember getting engaged," Ori said softly. "Do you want her to come out here? For the wedding?"

"Why?"

"She *is* your best friend. Even if you don't remember her."

"I know it's weird," I said. "Because at first, when I lost my memory, I would've done anything to get it back. I wanted to remember everything so badly. But now, I think, what's the point? So I can be sentimental? What if I'm not sentimental?"

"You're not sentimental," he interrupted. "You moved out of your father's house, and you took his desk, his liquor cart, and your bedroom furniture."

"That is now in the guest room at your house."

"Our house. It's our house now."

My hand searched for his. When I found it, I laced our fingers. "I think I just want to look forward, you know? When I marry you, I don't want anyone there from my past. On my wedding day, I don't want to think about the things and people I can't remember. I just want to be happy, Ori. And I don't think I will be if Shannon comes."

I couldn't even bring to mind a picture of her. We'd spoken on the phone once since my accident. She'd demanded Ori put me on the phone, so she could hear for herself how I was doing. She hadn't stirred anything inside of me. There was a reason I wasn't remembering.

I simply didn't want to.

The few flashes of memories had stopped, and with them, all my anxiety.

I looked over at Ori. He was watching me with a predatory stillness. I took a moment to gaze at his body. Golden skin, dark hair. Firm muscles, but not at all bulky.

"What?" Ori asked, reaching over and stroking my cheek.

"I was just thinking about how beautiful you are."

Pleasure at my compliment flared in his brown eyes.

"I was just thinking about how beautiful our children will be."

Pleasure turned to desire. He rolled over on top of me and smiled. "Let's find out, shall we?"

Chapter 26
SASHA

When I came face to face with Ori Abruzzo, I was going to strangle him with my bare hands.

"Another vodka, sir?" the flight attendant asked.

She was young and beautiful. At one time in my life, she would've given me the heavy-lidded stare, the one that said she wanted me. At one time in my life, I would've obliged.

But now, I was nothing more than a scarred man. She was a professional, so when she looked at me, her smile seemed genuine.

"Yes, I'll have another vodka," I said with a smile of my own. She flinched. It wasn't my fault the skin around my mouth pulled taut. She turned and went back behind the curtain, no doubt glad to escape me.

I had two hours before I landed in Rome. Two hours for Dimitri to get his shit together and call me. Because the moment I'd gotten on the plane, I'd realized I had no idea where to find Quinn. How the hell did you find an amnesiac that was engaged to a man she hardly knew?

I'd called Barrett from the tarmac to tell her the situation. After she'd flipped the fuck out over finding out Quinn was engaged, she'd told me she'd call her guy and have him do some digging of his own. That's why I loved Barrett—she had her own guy, a computer hacker from way back. Discreet and good at finding needles in haystacks.

I needed every bit of help I could get. But I'd rather hang around in Italy, so I could move when I needed to. Now an ocean no longer separated us.

According to Shannon, Quinn had just started dating Abruzzo. Something about this entire situation didn't sit right with me. I was missing something, I knew it. It was staring me in the face, and I couldn't see it because I was so close to it.

Why had Abruzzo whisked Quinn off to Italy? To keep her away from the people that knew her? What was he trying to pull? Was he after her money?

I cursed in Russian—out loud—just as the flight attendant returned with my vodka. Taking it from her with a smile, I turned to look out the window. We were among the clouds. I'd once felt like I'd lived among them, too. It was an illusion, of course. We weren't gods. When we fell, we hit the ground and our bodies shattered.

Hubris. It's why Igor had died.

I'd almost died, but it hadn't been because of hubris. It had been because of love—I'd saved the woman I loved, and now I'd save her again.

When I found her, I'd never let her go. I would force her to remember. I would hold her head, stare into her eyes, and bring back the memories of us. Every last painful, gut-wrenching memory. Because mixed up in all of that was love. Not just any sort of love, but the kind of love that would last a lifetime. The kind of love mere mortals dreamed of. The kind of love I'd cavalierly thrown away thinking I didn't deserve it.

I must've dozed, because the next thing I knew, we were descending. I swallowed the rest of the vodka and then handed the empty glass to the flight attendant. I hadn't been back in the States seventy-two hours, and already I was leaving again. My life was in a constant state of transition.

The plane landed and then rolled up to the gate. The intercom crackled, and then an attendant spoke in Italian, and then she switched to English. I was the first one off the plane since I had no carry-ons or luggage. I knew how it looked: scarred man without any sort of personal belongings. But customs gave me no trouble, and they waved me through. Perhaps they should've looked closer at the people entering their country.

I turned my phone on and had several missed messages. The first was from Dimitri. I called him back immediately.

"He doesn't exist," Dimitri said when he answered the phone.

"What does that mean?" I asked, heading to a somewhat secluded corner. Most patrons on my flight were exhausted businessmen who wanted to grab their luggage and get to their hotel. The terminal emptied quickly, but I still guarded my words.

"Ori Abruzzo. Doesn't exist. Sure, if you're a normal person, and you look him up on Facebook and the Internet, his picture shows up. He's got the obligatory profiles, but they're fake. Just enough so people don't look too closely."

"So who is he?"

"Don't know," Dimitri said with a sigh. "He's made himself untraceable. I'm going to need some more time."

"More time?" I snapped. "I'm in fucking Italy, I have no idea where Quinn is, and she's with a guy who I don't trust who's not even a real person? Who the fuck is he?"

"I can only do what I can do," Dimitri said, voice calm, placating. "I'm doing my best."

"Not good enough."

"You do not get to pull that shit with me, Sasha. You're the one who walked out and left us holding our own dicks."

"You did fine without me. You don't need me."

"You say that, you bastard. But you didn't just walk out on Quinn."

Shame, blistering hot shame, that neither time nor distance managed to dissipate, curled through my veins. "If he hurts her…"

"I know."

I sighed. "Take care, brother." I hung up and then called Barrett, not bothering to pause for breath.

"They flew into Pescara," she said before I could say anything.

"Pescara?"

"A city in the Abruzzo region. We tracked Quinn's passport in the system. If I had to guess, I'd say she's staying in the area."

"And where the fuck is Abruzzo?" I demanded, praying to a god I didn't believe in, hoping he'd throw me a fucking bone.

"Fifty miles east of Rome. But listen, my guy tried to find Ori, but his passport—"

"Untraceable?" I finished for her.

"Yeah. How'd you know?"

"Dimitri."

"Ah." She breathed a sigh of relief. "If you don't kill this Ori Abruzzo, I'll do it for you."

"Please tell me you're calling from a burner," I warned. "The last thing we need—"

"I've taken precautions. Don't you worry."

"Thanks, Barrett."

"Find her, Sasha."

"I will," I vowed.

Or I'd die trying.

Chapter 27

QUINN

I woke up to the scent of French toast. Rolling over, I forced my eyes open, unsure of the time. The sun was out and it was bright. It could've been late morning or early afternoon. I had no way of knowing. The last few days I'd been waking up in Boston to cold, dreary weather. I'd been forced to remain inside, but now all I wanted to do was explore.

My body was sore and achy, but in a way that told me I'd been well-loved the night before. I reached for Ori's white button-down shirt. I lifted it to my nose and inhaled the smell. His cologne lingered at the collar, and with a sigh, I threw it on.

I padded down the stairs. Every now and again one of them creaked, but it did nothing to hide the sound coming from the kitchen—Ori singing. Quietly, so as not to alert him, I stood in the doorway and watched him flip French toast onto plates and sing. I had no idea what song it was— it was in Italian—but he was wiggling his hips and using the spatula as an air guitar.

He turned off the burner and set the spatula down so

he could pick up a bowl filled with blackberries. As he dressed the plates of French toast and continued to dance and sing, it was harder and harder to stifle my laughter.

Finally, I couldn't contain it; I burst into a fit of giggles. Ori whirled, bowl of blackberries in his hand. His eyes widened.

"How long have you been there?" he demanded.

"Long enough." I shimmied toward him. "Gotta say. I'm a fan of the moves."

Ori quirked his lips into an amused grin. "Yeah? What about the ole pipes? How did you feel about them?"

I placed my hands on his chest and dragged them up his old faded T-shirt. The purple cotton was nearly threadbare. I felt the hard muscles beneath and then wrapped my arms around his neck and pressed against him.

"I'm into it," I said with a grin. "Good morning."

"Morning," he whispered gruffly as he kissed my lips. One arm came around me and hauled me closer. The other still held the blackberries. When he pulled back, he said, "I was going to bring you a plate in bed."

"This is better," I assured him.

He let me go and then playfully swatted my butt. "Get some coffee. Table's already set."

"How did you do all this?" I demanded as I moved past him toward the coffee pot. I poured a mugful and then doctored it heavily with cream and sugar. Apparently, my taste buds didn't have amnesia. They hated coffee but loved cream and sugar.

Ori took the two plates of French toast and headed for the table. "It's amazing what you can get done before eleven a.m."

I blinked. "It's eleven a.m.?"

"No, Quinn. It's not eleven a.m. It is now"—he glanced at his wristwatch—"eleven fifteen."

"What time were you up this morning?" I demanded, taking a seat. Leaning over, I closed my eyes and breathed in the smell of the French toast.

"Around eight." He took the blue napkin off the table and set it across his lap.

"We didn't go to bed until four."

"Four Italy time," he reminded me.

"How are you not wrecked right now?"

He grinned. "Eat your French toast before it gets cold."

I dutifully picked up my fork and knife. While I waited for him to answer, I cut a bite and stuck it into my mouth. I chewed and swallowed. "I am your humble slave."

"Good?" He raised an eyebrow, looking arrogant and sexy.

"Better than good. But I think you know that already."

We ate in silence. When food was that good, you didn't ruin it by talking. I savored every rich bite. The maple syrup combined with the tart blackberries had me in a near fit.

Half my mouth curved into a smile, and I shook my head.

"What?" Ori asked, setting his fork down on his empty plate.

"I was just thinking…I get to enjoy you cooking me breakfast for years to come."

"Yeah," Ori drawled. "You're pretty lucky."

I laughed. "What do I do for you? Huh? I don't cook. As you reminded me."

"You definitely don't cook. You"—he looked at me and reached out to catch my chin in his hand—"love me. And that's all you have to do, Quinn. Love me."

I turned my head, so my mouth grazed his palm. "I can do that."

He released me and then made a move to grab my

empty plate. I playfully slapped his hands away and took the plates to the sink to wash them by hand. The villa did not have a dishwasher. How anyone got away with entertaining was beyond me. "I want to see the town today."

"Really? You want to leave here? Leave the bed? I had plans for that bed."

"You always have plans with a bed," I teased.

Ori chuckled. "Actually, I was going to take you to meet my family."

One sudsy plate slipped out of my hand and landed in the porcelain sink and broke into two pieces. "Shit," I muttered, pulling the two halves out of the water and setting them on the counter. "How did that happen?"

"Those plates are about thirty years old," Ori said. "Don't worry about it. You cut yourself?"

"No."

"Then yeah, don't worry about it. If you look out the kitchen window, you can see those hills. Can't you?"

I dried my hands on a red and white striped dishtowel. "Yeah."

"That's my grandfather's vineyard. My mother's father," he clarified. "He's lived here his entire life. My mom was raised here. My mother's side of the family still lives here—in Abruzzo. I'd like for them to meet you."

"You want to introduce your big fat Italian family to the Irish girl you want to marry?"

He grinned. "What do you say? Are you up for it?"

"Do I look okay?" I asked, smoothing a hand down the navy–blue A-line dress I'd been smart enough to pack.

Ori popped his head through his gray sweater and smiled. "Beautiful. You're not going to be cold, are you? My grandfather likes to dine *al fresco*. Even in sixty-degree weather. As long as it's clear."

I bit my lip. "Yeah, I'll probably get cold, but what am I supposed to do?"

"Wear pants."

"Pants. To meet your family? I'm trying here, okay?"

He grinned.

"I'm guessing your family's a bit…old school?"

"You could say that."

"Then I'll wear the dress and be cold. It's just for a few hours."

"Right. A few hours." Ori blinked.

"What aren't you telling me?"

"Uh, we're not coming back until tomorrow."

"We're staying the night? Why?"

"My grandfather, he—just—I don't know. Likes it when the entire family is all together. And it doesn't happen frequently, what with my mom and sisters and me living in the States."

"So we're going to crash at your grandfather's house on what, a pullout sofa?"

Ori snorted. "Not a pullout sofa. In the guest room. Well, two guest rooms. We aren't actually *allowed* to sleep in the same room."

"Spell this out for me, because I am not getting it."

"Catholic. My family is Catholic and we're not—"

"Married," I finished for him. "Even though we're adults and living together."

"I know it's a lot to ask, but I want his blessing, ya know?"

"I guess." I frowned. I didn't understand the tradition, and it made me wonder about my own parents and how they would've handled Ori and us living together before marriage. Did people really still get hung up on that? Must've been a generational thing.

"What happens if you don't get his blessing?" I asked.

"I'll get it," he assured me.

"But if you don't."

"Then I'll marry you anyway."

"Go against your family? Bold move."

Ori paused. "My mother loves you."

"She does?" I breathed a sigh of relief. "That's good. Even though…crap."

"Even though you don't remember her?"

I shook my head. "Weird right?"

"No weirder than all the other stuff you don't recall."

"Fair point." I smiled, letting him know I didn't find that statement at all offensive. It was just the truth. And if you couldn't joke about amnesia with your future husband, who could you joke about it with?

I snorted at the thought. "Let's go. And just so you know I plan on charming the pants off your grandfather."

He headed for the bedroom door. "Please don't. He's old which means he's got knobby knees."

Ori drove us in a tiny car up a windy road through the hills. Mist settled among the trees. It was chilly, but it didn't detract from the beauty. Green. But not a bright green like in a country where it rained all the time, but darker, richer.

The vineyard had looked deceptively close when seen through the kitchen window of the villa. But in fact, it was a good thirty minutes away. Nestled on the side of a hill. And instead of a quaint villa that I had expected, the home was a mansion. An Italian mansion, but a mansion all the same.

I peered at Ori. "Your family certainly has done well for itself."

He smiled as he parked. "We have. The Abruzzos have prospered over the years." He was out of the car before I even had my seatbelt unlatched. The front door of the house opened and about fifteen people spilled out of the entrance. I watched as Ori's family embraced him. The women with dark hair and dark eyes pinched his cheeks. He smiled good-naturedly and took it. The men embraced him and then the kids crowded around. A little girl with curly dark hair down to the middle of her back ran toward him, and Ori lifted her in the air high above his head. The little girl giggled.

It was one of those moments that froze in time, when I could picture how he'd look throwing his own child up over his head, his smile pure, effortless. It made me yearn for all the things that hadn't yet come. It made me lament all the memories that were missing.

Burning tears formed in my eyes, but I quickly brushed them away. Now was not the time to let emotion get the best of me.

Ori set the little girl down. I thought she'd run back toward the other children, but instead, she grasped onto Ori's hand and pointed at me. He crouched down so he was at eye level with her. Ori said something to her, and she nodded. Before I knew it, they were stalking toward me.

"Quinn," Ori began, "I want you to meet Alessandra. Alessandra, this is Quinn." He repeated the introduction in Italian.

"Nice to meet you," I said, holding out my hand to the girl who couldn't have been more than five. She stared up at me with luminous dark brown eyes, clutching a stuffed animal that might have at one time been a rabbit. She smiled and took my hand with her tiny one.

After she shook my hand, she rescinded it and then clutched Ori's leg and hid behind it, peeking up at me.

"I want five just like her," I said to Ori, keeping my smile in place.

Ori chuckled. "Heard loud and clear, *Cerbiatto*."

The Italian word had Alessandra tittering and then saying something in the same language. Ori replied, and then the girl dashed away.

"What was that about?" I asked.

"She asked if you were my girlfriend. I set her straight."

Ori wrapped his arm around me and guided me toward the expectant family waiting to meet me. For some reason they were showing great restraint. Maybe they didn't want to overwhelm me?

Ori looked down at me and then said, "You ready?"

"For what?"

Ori spoke in Italian, and the only word I recognized was my name. And then the family was upon me.

I'd never been happier.

Chapter 29

QUINN

Something happened when you didn't understand a foreign language. You didn't worry about what others said about you. I sat at a long wooden table, my plate loaded with Italian delicacies. Antipasti of meats and cheeses, olives, peppers. And any time I took a sip of wine, someone was there to fill it up.

Ori had warned me we'd be dining outside. We sat under a canopy attached to the house. Ori was by my side, his hand resting on my thigh, his other arm around me. He leaned over and opened his mouth, and I plopped a grape into it. Once he finished chewing, he kissed my temple and turned his attention back to his uncle who hadn't taken a breath in fifteen minutes.

The patriarch of the family still hadn't made his appearance. I was starting to worry he didn't think I was good enough for his grandson and that was the reason he hadn't come down to eat.

Finally, the elusive man graced us with his presence—and he wasn't at all like Ori described him. His grandfather was tall, stately, with a full head of white hair and a stoic expression. He wore gray slacks and a red sweater, his dark brown eyes surveying the entire family from underneath bushy salt and pepper eyebrows.

The entire table fell silent.

His grandfather's gaze rested on Ori who slowly removed himself from my side and stood. The two men faced each other, looking more like adversaries than family. But the old man's face cracked, and a wide smile took over. He spoke in rapid Italian and moved toward us. He embraced Ori, holding on tightly. When he released him, his eyes slid to mine.

I smiled tremulously. He patted his chest and said, "*Nonno.*"

Frowning in confusion, I looked up at Ori.

"Italian for Grandfather."

"*Nonno,*" I repeated with a nod.

Nonno pulled me against him, and I fell into his chest with an *oof.* Everyone around the table started talking again, so it no longer felt like I was on full display.

When I pulled back, I smiled.

Nonno dropped my hands, and Ori wrapped his arm around me and pulled me into his side. Ori spoke in Italian and Nonno nodded, shooing us away. His grandfather reached down to my plate and plucked an olive from it. He popped it into his mouth and chewed a moment before spitting the pit out into his hand.

Ori leaned around him and took his wine glass and gave it to Nonno. Nonno drank the wine like it was water. Or sparkling water.

"Where are we going?" I asked as Ori tugged me toward the house. I pitched my voice lower. "You're not taking me somewhere for a quickie, are you?"

He threw me a grin over his shoulder. "In my grandfather's home? Yeah, I don't think so. Do you know how many Virgin Mary paintings he has in this house? Thirty-seven."

"Yikes. So where are we going?"

"I'm going to show you the vineyard."

We trekked through the house, and Ori opened the door, which dumped us on the side of his grandfather's home. It was chilly, and the mist settled even more, giving the vineyard an ethereal mystical quality.

"Are you sure this is a good idea?" I asked. "It's hard to see…"

Ori bent down and tugged off one of his shoes and put on a boot. "Yeah, this is a good idea. I know these rows. I could walk them blind. Take off your heels; they're not walking shoes." He handed me a masculine pair of black rubber boots, smaller than the ones he was wearing.

I didn't fight him and kicked off my heels and pulled on the boots. "How do I look?" I asked, posing.

"Like a young Sophia Loren," he teased.

"Who?"

"Never mind." He held out his hand, and I grasped it. We walked down the small hill toward the vines. The rubber boots were a bit too big, so they rubbed at my ankles and calves.

"How are you doing?" Ori asked. His fingers tightened around mine as he continued to lead me across his grandfather's property.

"With?"

"My family. Are they at least trying to speak English?"

"Sometimes," I said. "But it's kind of fun when they speak Italian. You can tell a lot by watching people, you know? Language barrier or not. They love you."

"Yes, they do. They'll love you too."

"Learning Italian might speed up the process."

"You'd learn Italian?" he asked in surprise.

"Absolutely."

He drew me into the side of his body and brushed his lips against my cheek. "Well, what do you think?"

We stopped walking so I could take in the rolling hills. "I think this is incredible," I marveled. I could picture it. Summers in Abruzzo, children running through the lanes of the vineyard, their laughter echoing through the trees.

"Why is your last name the same as the region?"

"My mother's family is from the Abruzzi, a mountainous region of Italy east of Rome. Our last name is just a variation."

I took a moment to digest his explanation. "Was I close to my parents?" I asked suddenly. "I mean, I know my mother died when I was in high school…but my father. Was I close to him?"

"Very."

"Was I lonely? Before you?"

"Yes." His voice was a whisper, an ache.

I smiled and looked up at him. "I want to live loud. Does that make sense?"

"It does." He brought our hands to his lips and brushed his mouth against the tender skin of my palm. "Let's go back. I'm ready for tiramisu."

Chapter 30
QUINN

We headed back to the house and slipped inside, undetected. The family was still out front enjoying the meal. I brushed my lips against Ori's and said, "I need to use the restroom."

"Top of the stairs, make a left," he said, kissing me again but making it quick.

"Save me a slice of tiramisu."

"No promises." He winked and then went to spend time with his family.

With a dreamy sigh, I turned toward the staircase. My hand glided up the smooth wooden railing as I took the stairs slowly. Pictures dotted the wall, and soon I was lost in the family's story. Paintings turned to black and white photography and then black and white turned to color. I saw the wedding photo of a young Nonno and his wife. They were smiling, a beautiful couple in love. When I got to the top of the stairs, I was just about to turn toward the bathroom when a framed photograph caught my eye. It was a picture of Ori as a teenager. He was a lanky kid, his dark hair falling across his forehead, but even then I could see he was handsome. He was in the photo with two other boys his age. The one in the middle, my eyes slid over. It was the boy on the far right that caught my attention. Athletic build, high cheekbones and penetrating ice blue eyes.

Frowning, I inched closer to the frame. There was something about that boy… something that pulled at a memory deep in my mind.

"He is a handsome boy, no?" a woman said.

I visibly jumped. I hadn't heard her approach and tried to curb the rapid beat of my heart. "Uh, yes he is." I cocked my head to the side. "You speak English well."

The woman smiled and adjusted the sleepy toddler on her hip. Dark hair flowed down her back, but she didn't have the same look as the other Abruzzos. "I studied for a time in the States. Most of the family speaks English, but they would rather not." She rubbed the back of the sleeping baby. "I'm Camilla, Ori's second cousin."

"Did we meet downstairs?"

She shook her head. "This one is running a slight fever. So I've been with him up here. He's finally sleeping which is good."

I peered down at the flushed cheeks of her son. He was beautiful, with a mop of dark curls and a cupid bow mouth. I smiled and then my attention turned back to the photo of three teenage boys.

"Who's with Ori in those photos?"

"Ah." She pointed to the boy in the middle, her fingernail tapping the glass. "This is Igor. He was Ori's best friend."

"Was?"

Camilla nodded. "He died. Six years ago, I think. Ori was really torn up about it. He and Igor were inseparable."

I forced my voice to sound calm, casual, but my heart was thundering in my chest like a band of horses. "Who's the other boy?" I asked.

"Sasha. Igor's other best friend."

Sasha.

The name reverberated through me, settling in the pit of my stomach. My palms were suddenly cold and clammy. "What happened to him?" My voice sounded far away to me but somehow calm.

"I don't know," Camilla said. "Ori doesn't talk about Sasha. Not after Igor's sudden death."

"How'd Igor die?" I asked, avid curiosity churning inside of me.

"He was shot."

My heart ached for Ori. Instead of saying anything, I looked away from Camilla and back to the framed photograph.

Sasha wasn't a common name. The man I'd been with before Ori had been named Sasha. I was starting to think coincidences didn't exist. But I wanted time by myself to process before asking Ori if the Sasha in the photograph was the man I'd once been with.

"Well," I said, shaking my head. "I was on the way to the restroom. Better take care of that before Ori sends a search party."

Camilla laughed softly so as not to disturb her son. "He is a bit overprotective of you."

"You think so?" I asked, forcing a sideways smile. All I wanted was to get away, but I didn't want Camilla to look too closely at me.

"Well, knowing your circumstances…I guess not."

"The amnesia thing, you mean?" When she nodded, I went on. "It was smothering, at first. When I wasn't— when I'd just gotten out of the hospital. I just needed to breathe, but Ori didn't leave my side. He respected my needs and then"—I shrugged—"I don't know. I realized I liked his attention. In that way."

"He really does love you," she said.

"I know. I love him too."

"How?"

I frowned. "What do you mean?"

"If you can't remember him, how can you be in love with him?"

"Because I've fallen in love with Ori all over again. Whatever we had before… I don't remember."

"You can't fall in love with someone in a few days."

"*You* can't, maybe," I said, refusing to back down from her bluntness. "But if you'd known how he—never mind."

"Finish that sentence," she commanded.

Her demand didn't faze me. Nor did I feel inclined to listen. "I get that you're family and you're just trying to protect him, but you don't have anything to fear from me."

Camilla peered at me with dark brown eyes. "You can't remember your past, which tells me you probably don't remember Ori's past. What he's shared with you, what he hasn't. I love him. We all love him. We just don't want you to cause him any more pain."

I looked back at the photograph. Three young boys. One of them dead, the other not spoken of. I looked at Ori's smile. So wide and bright. Hopeful.

I wanted to learn everything there was to know about Ori and his past. I didn't care to remember mine, not when I knew it harbored such sadness. What good would it do? But I hadn't thought about Ori's past and if it was full of his own sadness and losses.

"How do I make him smile like that?" I pointed to the photo. "I'll do anything to see that smile."

Camilla cocked her head to one side. "Don't you know? You already do make him smile like that. Which is why we're terrified you'll ruin him."

Chapter 31
QUINN

Camilla finally released me from her pointed questions, and I escaped to the bathroom. All I wanted to do was curl up in a guest room and ponder the Sasha of Ori's past from the Sasha of mine.

What if they were the same person?

Why wouldn't Ori have told me that they knew each other? What did that mean?

I would get no answers from hiding in a bedroom, so I forced myself to return to the table. Ori was sitting with a glass of wine in one hand and smiling and talking with his grandfather. When he saw me, Ori winked and then patted the seat next to him. I ignored the family's collective eyes on me and walked over to him. I grasped his glass of wine and took a hearty sip.

"You're not supposed to drink," he reminded me.

"I'm in Italy. And I've been drinking all day." I leaned close to his ear so no one else would hear me when I said, "And your family is a pack of Italian hyenas."

Ori's eyes glimmered with humor. I sat next to Ori and

gave Nonno a wide smile. His gaze tracked me, even lingering on the glass of wine that I'd filched from Ori.

"What are you guys talking about?" I asked.

"Just catching up," Ori said. "Telling him about the family in the States."

Someone set a slice of tiramisu in front of me. I reached for the spoon and zoned out, listening to the chatter of soft Italian words around me. The afternoon wore on into evening and soon people were leaving, wanting to get their tired children into their own beds.

I needed my bed, too. The jet lag had finally gotten to me. And smiling and laughing all afternoon had taken its toll. Not to mention the thoughts weighing on my mind.

After saying our goodbyes to the family, Ori took me upstairs to the guest room. My overnight bag, which I'd packed that morning, was resting at the foot of the bed.

"We really can't go back to your villa?" I asked, unzipping the bag and searching for my pajamas.

"And offend my grandfather?"

"Any chance he sleeps like a hibernating bear so you can sneak into my room and—"

"I'm begging you not to finish that sentence. Because I'm already finding it incredibly difficult to walk out of here."

"Tell him if he lets us sleep together then he can expect a great-grandchild in about nine months."

"You're killing me, Quinn." He grinned. "Listen, I have to leave you with my family tomorrow."

I found the pajamas and pulled them out. "Why?"

"Because I have to take care of some paperwork—legal paperwork to make sure we can get married."

"You're not trying to get a quickie Italian divorce, are you?"

Ori laughed. "Not even close. There's just a lot of red

tape when two Americans who don't live in Italy want to get married here. And I'd kind of like to make sure that when we get married, it's legal, ya know?"

"That would be nice," I said with a smile.

"So, I guess I have to ask…"

"Ask what?" I dove back into my bag, wanting to find my toothbrush.

"Are you going to change your last name?"

"Yeah, of course." I dug deeper into the bag. "Damn it, seriously where's my toothbrush? I thought I'd put it on top."

"Quinn?"

"Yeah."

"Can you look at me?"

Frowning in confusion, I looked up at him. "What's up?"

He stalked toward me and cradled my cheeks in his hands. "Thank you."

"For what?"

"For wanting to take my name."

"I don't get it."

"It just—it means a lot to me." He placed his lips on mine, and then his tongue was in my mouth, kissing me breathless. I wanted more, but I also wanted space. I still didn't have the courage to ask him about Sasha. I had a feeling if I asked him, it would taint our happiness—and I didn't want to spoil it.

"So while you're off doing all that, what am I supposed to do?"

He grinned and his hands left my face. "Plan the wedding."

"Plan the wedding. Oh, sure."

"My cousins will help."

"Uh huh."

"You're going to need a dress, Quinn."

I crossed my arms over my chest. "Doesn't seem fair, Ori. I have to handle all that stuff while you—"

"Find the right officials to pay off to speed up the marriage license paperwork. We could switch jobs if you want."

"Fine, fine. I'll do all the preparations. Do I have a time frame?"

"End of the week. It's not that hard to plan a wedding, Quinn. There's only going to be about fifty guests."

I rolled my eyes. "You really have no idea, do you? You're such a man."

He swatted me on the butt.

"Get out of here," I said with a laugh. "Before your grandfather comes in and cuts off your—"

"I'm going, I'm going." With one last kiss, he sauntered toward the door. "Oh, and Quinn?"

"Yeah?"

He looked over his shoulder and grinned. "Don't forget to buy some lingerie."

Chapter 32

QUINN

I awoke in the middle of the night disoriented, a bad dream lingering in my mind. I couldn't remember what I'd been dreaming about, yet I was left with feelings of sadness and shattering loneliness.

Throwing off the covers, I inhaled a deep breath. I clambered out of bed, feeling a tad woozy. Dehydration and wine were making their effects known. On my way out of the room, I bashed my knee against the heavy wooden chest I'd forgotten was on the floor at the base of the bed.

Wincing, I gave it a good rub, and when the stinging dissipated, I continued. The house was dark and silent. I crept downstairs, planning on rooting around in the kitchen, but came to a stop when I heard the gentle hum of soft voices.

I would've gone back to bed, but curiosity got the better of me. After inching closer, I hid in the shadows.

"We can speak in Italian," Ori said with gentle humor. "If you'd prefer."

Nonno laughed. "My English is rusty."

I blinked. The man spoke English without a trace of an Italian accent. What the hell?

"If you say so. Your English sounds fine to me."

"There is always room for improvement. A concept lost on your generation."

"Here we go," Ori said with a laugh.

Nonno switched to Italian, his words causing Ori to laugh again.

"Should we get down to it?" Nonno asked, reverting back to English.

"Yeah."

"The Drugovs are ready to make their move."

"Are they?" Ori said, his voice steely. "I'm not ready."

"The girl…"

"Her name is Quinn, Nonno."

"Is she what you want?"

"Yes."

"More than revenge?"

I inhaled a sharp breath and was instantly worried that they'd heard me. I pressed a hand to my mouth. I wanted to continue eavesdropping on their conversation, but then I heard one of them get up.

I quickly turned around and headed up the stairs. I got into bed and pulled the covers up to my chin.

Ori spoke of revenge. What did that mean? And who were the Drugovs? My mind flashed to the photo on the wall of the three boys. Igor, Ori, and Sasha. Two of those names were Russian.

The door to my bedroom creaked open. I feigned sleepiness, despite the fact that my pulse was on overdrive. "Ori?" I whispered.

"Did I wake you?" he asked, coming to the side of the bed.

"No. I—I had a bad dream," I said.

Ori crawled underneath the covers and pulled me into his arms. "Tell me about it."

"I don't remember. What are you doing? I thought you couldn't—"

"Shhhh." His hands began to wander and despite my uneasiness of what I'd heard downstairs, I let him touch me and bring me pleasure. I even welcomed him into my body and held him close as he fell asleep. Even though I was confused. Even though I wasn't sure I trusted him.

I listened to the sound of Ori's breathing. Whenever I tried to get out of bed, he would clutch me in his sleep, like he was afraid to lose me.

How stupid was I?

To marry a man when I didn't know who I was—or who he was. Apparently. Because I wasn't getting the feeling that Ori was just another businessman or that his grandfather was an old Italian man who owned a vineyard.

Normal people didn't speak of revenge.

What didn't I know? What did I want to uncover?

I finally conked out around dawn but woke up only a few hours later to Ori kissing me goodbye. "I should be back by early evening."

"Should be?" I asked.

"Yeah. If it all goes according to plan. I'll meet you back at the villa. After you're done today in town, just have Camilla drop you off."

He kissed me again and looked like he never wanted to leave my side. What was he hiding? What didn't he want me to know?

Why was I afraid to ask him?

Ori finally left. I leaned back against the pillows of the bed, planning on catching a few more minutes of sleep. Just as my eyes were drifting shut, the door to the room burst open. Camilla and a few other women ran inside, chattering in Italian and pulling the covers off me.

"What's happening?" I demanded.

"Get in the shower," Camilla said. "We'll have breakfast after, and then we're headed to town."

I blinked, sluggish. Why did I have a feeling that I was just along for the ride? When Ori told me to plan our wedding, he really meant not to get in the way of his cousins who would plan our wedding.

"What size bra do you wear?" Camilla called through the closed door of the bathroom. "You know what, you should just let me measure." She tried to open the door, but I threw the lock.

"No measurements until after coffee!" I called back.

Camilla laughed. "The measurements are the least of your worries today."

I'd been to three towns already, holding up my phone with a picture of Quinn and discretely asking questions. No one had seen her, so I'd driven on. I hadn't slept in eighteen hours, and I was running on vodka fumes and caffeine. And adrenaline. I could crash when she was in my grasp, when she was safe, and I'd gotten her away from Ori Abruzzo.

I didn't expect to get lucky because luck was never on my side. But apparently, luck had a change of heart, because the cold-hearted bitch dragged me to a café in a tiny town in Pescara that I couldn't pronounce. As I was sipping my second espresso hoping for a refuel, I heard two middle-aged women talking in fluid Italian at the table next to me. I was just getting ready to ask for the check, when I caught the name Ori Abruzzo and the word *matrimonio*.

That bastard was planning on marrying Quinn as fast as possible. His death was going to be slow. So agonizingly slow. He was preying on Quinn, who had no memory. He was using it against her, manipulating her into a situation she never would have entered into if she had all her faculties.

They got up, grabbed their purses and wandered toward the flower shop around the corner. I waited until they were gone to call Barrett.

"I found her," I said.

"And? Did you talk to her?"

"It's not like that. But I'm in a town in Pescara, and I just heard two women mention Ori Abruzzo and a wedding."

"Wedding? You're kidding. What's your plan?"

"How soon can you get here?"

"Me? What do you need me for?"

"Back up."

"Are we just supposed to do an old-school Bonnie and Clyde stake out?" she asked.

"Didn't they both die?"

"Bad example," she said with a sigh. "Flynn's not going to let me come alone."

"So bring him along."

"Just when I thought we would be able to curl up in front of the fire and read our children bedtime stories. Remind me to write a book called *Mafia Meets Motherhood*. I think it would sell well in our circle."

I laughed. "Just get your ass on a plane."

"Only if you ask nicely."

"Barrett," I growled, no longer in the mood to tease.

"Your wish is my command."

She hung up. I reached into my pocket to grab my wallet, set a few Euros on the table, and went in the direction of the two women, hoping they'd talk to me.

Chapter 34

QUINN

After breakfast, the girls took me into town and all but shoved me through the door of the wedding dress boutique.

"You ready to try on some wedding dresses?" Camilla asked.

"Sure," I said in a complete daze.

Nodding, she spoke to the assistant in Italian. Hands came about from nowhere, herding me to a changing room. I felt like a twig swept along with the rushing river. There was no hope of stopping it. I was Ori Abruzzo's bride, and apparently his female cousins had a vision for how his bride was supposed to look on her wedding day.

But I was lucky, because the first dress I tried on was the one. The Italian lace slid across my skin. It was beautiful and decadent. The silhouette was a classic sheath, covering me from neck to wrist. It was form fitting, sexy yet demure. The matching veil draped down my back.

When I looked in the mirror and stared at my reflection, I tried to picture Ori in a tux standing next to me.

I heard my name being called and a knock. I reached

over and unlocked the door to open it, pasting a smile on my face. "This is the one," I said.

Camilla and the others fell silent as they gaped at me in my wedding dress. Finally, Camilla nodded. "That is the dress. Yes. Absolutely."

They helped me out of the garment and took it to the cash register. I dressed slowly, wondering how the hell I was going to escape their clutches. I needed time to myself. They were smothering me.

I got out of the dressing room just as the attendant was taking the dress toward the back to wrap. It was a beautiful gown. Delicate. Perfect.

The sight of it made me sick.

"Are you okay?" Camilla asked.

"Hmm? Oh, yeah."

"You sure? You look pale."

"I'm getting a headache," I said, which wasn't a lie at all. The throb began at my temples.

"Do you usually get headaches?" Camilla wondered.

"How the hell am I supposed to know?" I snapped. "I have amnesia. Can someone please drive me back to the villa?"

"Do you have medicine?"

I nodded. "The doctor prescribed it to me after the accident. It's at Ori's villa."

"I'll drive you."

Since we'd all piled into three separate cars, it wasn't a problem splitting off from the rest of Ori's cousins. I climbed into the passenger side of the compact blue car and leaned my head against the cool glass. My headache had gone from a dull throb to a full-blown pounding and with it came the nausea. Not two minutes into the drive, I commanded, "Pull over. I'm going to throw up."

Camilla stopped the car, and I opened the door just in

time. As I wiped my mouth, I leaned back against the seat, exhausted and still in pain. I managed to get the door closed, and then we drove away again.

It seemed to take forever to get back to the villa. Camilla helped me inside and guided me to the bedroom. I collapsed onto the bed as she drew the curtains of the windows shut, bathing me in darkness.

"Where's your medication?" she asked, her voice a whisper.

It still reverberated through my skull. My head felt like a bell someone had rung. "Bathroom," I said into the pillow.

A few minutes later, Camilla came back with a glass of water and two pills. I somehow sat up and forced down the horse pills. I didn't even bother crawling under the covers.

"Thanks," I said. I licked my lips. "Italian tap water tastes funny."

"Just rest, Quinn. Your headache will be gone soon."

Her words sounded far away, and before I knew it, I was sliding down into a dark tunnel, and then I knew nothing.

Chapter 35
QUINN

"You're the most beautiful thing I've ever seen," he said, his ice blue eyes dipping down my body. "What's it like?"

"What's what like?" I asked with a smirk.

"What's it like sitting in a vat of vodka wearing nothing but pearls?"

I was still wearing the pearls from the photo shoot. I was now the face of Krasnyy, the high-end vodka produced by my boyfriend—the Russian mafia king of Manhattan.

My fingers played with the warm beads, drawing his attention, drawing his desire. I spread my legs, showing him the heat of me. We'd just finished making love in his bed, but it had only stoked the flames.

Sometimes, he took me with a ferocious want, like a beast, like a warrior of old. Other times, he lingered over my taste, braising my skin with his love.

I wanted him any way I could have him.

I reached up and dragged my fingers down the side of his face. His high cheekbones were all Slavic ancestry.

"Quinn? Are you going to answer my question?" he asked in

amusement, his own hand seeking the curve of my hip. When he was inside me, he placed his hand there, like an anchor.

"It felt"—I searched for the right word—"decadent. Like who has that kind of money to just throw away for an artistic spread in a magazine?"

His mouth quirked up into an amused, arrogant grin. "Me."

I laughed. "Of course, you. I feel like part of me is supposed to be repulsed by the opulent wealth and the blatant disregard for the rules you don't have to follow."

"You don't have to follow them either, you know. Not as my woman."

"Your woman?" I raised my eyebrows. "A bit caveman, don't you think?"

"What about wife?" His blue eyes delved into mine as his fingers traced their own path down my thigh, dancing across my skin to play at the heat of me. "Would you prefer to be my wife?"

My heart tripped. "Is this your idea of a marriage proposal?"

His finger slid inside me, causing my head to fall back and a moan to spring to my lips. "Da, Quinn. This is my idea of a marriage proposal. Are you going to give me an answer?"

My eyes opened into slits. My body was on fire, begging for release. I grinned. "Make me come, and then I'll give you my answer."

He added another finger. It was both a punishment and a blessing. "Tell me, Quinn," he growled. "And then I'll make you come so hard you see stars."

I gripped his shoulders and pulled him to me so I could place my lips on his, suck his tongue into my mouth, absorb every piece of him so I didn't know where he ended, and I began.

"Yes, Sasha Petrovich, I'll marry you."

And then I didn't see stars, but an entire galaxy.

My eyes opened to a white ceiling. I remembered falling asleep to the shut curtains, sleeping in utter darkness. Someone must've opened them because I could see everything now. Including the man who sat on the edge of my bed.

Dark hair. Dark eyes.

"How do you feel?" Ori asked, face wreathed with concern. "Quinn?"

I glanced at my arm. An IV.

"What happened?" I croaked.

"You tell me. I found your pill bottle next to the bed."

I frowned. "I took two."

Ori's eyes narrowed. "You sure?"

"Yeah, I'm sure. I know how to count. What the hell is all this?"

"I came home early, and when I couldn't wake you up, I called the doctor."

"A doctor who makes house calls? Explains the IV," I muttered. "I took two pills, Ori. I swear."

He looked away from me to stare out the window. "Tell me what happened." His voice was soft, curious.

"We were at the wedding dress shop," I said. "And I got a bad headache. Out of nowhere."

He slowly turned his head to look at me. And then he waited for the rest of the story.

"Camilla drove me back here. I got into bed, she brought me two pills, and I took them." I fell silent, my mind whirling with thoughts. "The water," I said suddenly. "Something was in the glass of water she gave me. I remember it tasted funny. Tangy."

My eyes met his. They darkened with anger and firm resolution. "I'll handle this."

"Handle what exactly?" I asked, my gaze flitting across his face. He rose slowly to loom over me. "Ori?"

Gone was the affable, smiling man. In his place was a protector. A man I didn't recognize. "I hired a nurse to watch over you. If you need anything, ring the bell."

"Where are you going?" I demanded.

His eyes glittered with dangerous intent. "Out." He disappeared through the doorframe and shut the door.

What had just happened? And why did Ori suddenly terrify me?

Chapter 36
SASHA

Three hours later, I walked to a wedding boutique. The sun was setting and the shop assistant was locking the front door. She was a beautiful woman, lithe, graceful with the light coloring belonging to the Northern Italians.

"Excuse me," I said.

She turned her head. Her eyes took me in—from the burned face to the form concealed in a suit. "May I help you?"

"I was wondering if we could speak. Discreetly."

Her eyes narrowed in suspicion.

I held my hands up. "I swear, I'm not here to rob you. I just have a few questions I was hoping you could answer."

Whatever she saw on my face made her decide to unlock the door and push it open. She flipped on the lights as I trailed behind her. She closed the front door and locked it. Then she went to draw the shade on the door.

"What can I do for you?" she asked when she appeared confident that no one walking by would see her speaking with me.

"I was wondering if you could tell me if this woman

has been in your shop." I pulled out my phone, swiped it, and then flipped it around to show her a picture of Quinn.

"She was here. I don't know anything about her," she said, eyes lifting from the photo.

"I think you do," I said. "This is a small town, and this woman is clearly a foreigner. And this shop has been here for three generations. Which tells me you know things."

"Been doing some scouting, have you?" She raised a light, elegant eyebrow.

"I have been."

"Not enough, clearly. This town belongs to them."

"And you fear them, right? Because you don't want to talk to me."

"Someone will see me speaking to you. As you pointed out this is a small town. Foreigners stand out."

"I know they're getting married at the end of the week. Where?"

She named a church. "Do you plan on stopping the wedding?"

"Perhaps." I smirked but then sobered.

The woman looked away from my eyes to stare at a spot behind me. "They may run this town, but they haven't been good to my family."

Ah, family vendettas. You could always play them against one another.

"Be careful of the Marinos. They're snakes in the grass."

I frowned. "Marinos? I thought this town was run by the Abruzzos."

She made a noise of derision. "The Abruzzos are Marino puppets. Have been ever since they joined their families."

Blood rushed through my veins. "Ori Abruzzo—"

"Ori Abruzzo Marino," she clarified. "The heir apparent."

~

Ori Marino.

The son of Giovanni Marino—the man Campbell and I had set up to turn into the FBI. Only, that night on the docks, the plan had gone to shit and Marino had wound up dead. I'd taken over Italian territory to divert money to the SINS.

Ori Marino.

Igor's best friend from when we were teenagers.

The missing puzzle piece I couldn't seem to find finally fit into place. It all made sense now. This was planned, orchestrated. Years in the making. Marino wanted to take me down for killing his father and his best friend.

It was like a fist reached into my chest and started squeezing my heart. The bastard had Quinn. Quinn who couldn't remember her past. He was using her to find me.

I had to get to her, get her away from Marino and take her someplace safe where I could help her get her memories back.

I stopped walking. I was lost down a dark alleyway; I'd been trying to head back to the town square.

They came out of the stones. Paid assassins. My mind cleared and calm settled over me.

They were no match for what I'd become. I dispatched them easily, without breaking my knuckles or getting blood on my clothes.

Ori Marino had sent two killers, not to actually kill me, but to send me a message. To tell me that he knew I was here, in his town.

"Come and get me, fucker," I whispered.

Camilla had put something in my water. I knew that for sure. What I didn't understand was why? Why did she hate me and yet help me plan my wedding to Ori?

It didn't make sense.

I had my assumptions, of course, about Ori's family, about who they were and what they did. But for some reason, it felt all too familiar, being with a man who appeared to be one thing but was quite another.

Would Ori ever tell me what he was hiding from me? Would he ever tell me how Sasha factored into all of this? Or would he keep me in the dark?

I needed my memories back. I wanted to know myself and know him. I was tying my life to his; I'd have his children. I deserved to know the kind of man their father would be.

My head started pulsing again, so I forced myself to calm down. No use getting another migraine. That would slow me down, and I didn't have a moment to spare.

My phone.

The guy from the cell phone store told me how to

unlock it without remembering the password. I needed a computer and a chord. Ori had brought a laptop with him, and it was in the living room. I wanted to get out of bed, but the IV needle in my arm stopped me.

There was a knock and then a middle-aged woman came in carrying a tray. "Good, you're awake," she said in English. Her smile bloomed across her face.

"When can I remove the IV?"

"In a few hours. You really need to rest."

"I feel fine," I lied. I was woozy and a tad lightheaded.

"Can't fool me, young lady."

I wrinkled my nose at the *young lady*, but otherwise stayed silent.

"I brought you some toast and a little bit of broth. Just something easy on the belly." She set the tray down on top of my lap. "Can I get you anything else?"

"My cell phone," I said with a smile. "It's in my purse in the front room."

"I'll bring it to you," she said. "My name is Millie if you need anything." Before I could say thank you, Millie left. She came back almost immediately and handed over my purse. I dug through it and pulled out my cell.

"Thanks," I said to her with a smile.

"Get some rest," she said and closed the door on her way out.

I set the cell phone aside. It wasn't the one I was looking for. When it was clear that I wasn't able to remember my password, Ori had gotten me a new phone so I could reach him. So I'd been carting around two cell phones. Only my original cell phone wasn't in my purse.

It was missing.

Nausea surged in my stomach. Ori had taken it. I knew it. I knew it with every fiber of my being.

My name is Quinn O'Malley.

I was in a car accident.
I am engaged to a man keeping secrets from me.

I had no clue how long it would take for Ori to come back. I didn't waste any time and ripped the needle from my arm. Wincing, I managed to keep any sound of pain from escaping my lips. As I pulled on my clothes, I grew light-headed. Most people who'd just had their stomach pumped would probably wait, but they weren't in my circumstances—an amnesiac engaged to a very dangerous man who was probably a criminal. Not to mention related to a crazy woman who'd drugged me.

I went to the door of the bedroom and slowly turned the knob. Due to the villa's layout, I had a direct view into the living room. Millie was on the couch. The TV was on, and judging by the angle of her head, she'd dozed off.

Closing the door, I sent up a silent prayer. I went over to the window and unlocked it. I grabbed my purse, glad that I had my passport and credit cards. The late afternoon sun was hiding behind the clouds, and it was chilly, but at least it didn't look like rain. I managed to climb through the window and drop onto the ground.

Thank God for Italian villa floor plans.

When Ori had shown me the villa and the surrounding area, he'd pointed out a small shed, and inside were two bicycles. They looked like they belonged in the 1950s. I checked the tires and took the bike that was sound.

I put my purse in the bicycle basket and slowly guided it out of the shed. I closed the door and then maneuvered the bike around the side of the villa, hoping Millie was still asleep. If she caught me, I was a dead woman. She'd call Ori and tell him.

And the last thing I wanted was Ori to know that I was leaving. I didn't know where I was going or who I could trust. I didn't have any of my own memories, only a gut reaction that something was off. This whole thing was off.

Sunlight caught the edge of the diamond on my engagement band, and it shot a prism onto the side of the house. At any other time, I would've stopped to admire it, maybe even thought it was a sign, a hopeful sign that marriage to Ori would be full of light and beauty.

But I wasn't much for signs these days, and I'd been ignoring my instincts, shoving them down because for a few moments, I'd felt happy. He'd wanted me out of Boston. He'd wanted me tucked away here, in this tiny Italian village. He took my cell phone so on the off chance I did remember myself and our life together, I wouldn't have access to my past.

He'd cut me off. Or tried to.

I didn't know why he'd done it, but I wasn't sticking around to find out.

Rounding the corner of the villa, I was prepared to climb onto the bike and ride away, ride toward town where I could catch a cab and book it to the airport.

But I didn't count on Ori Abruzzo being one step ahead of me, and I came face to face with the man himself.

His body was taut, alert, a feral grin on his face. "Going somewhere?"

Chapter 38

SASHA

"You'd think with your own private plane you would've been here sooner," I stated.

Barrett hugged me. "Good to see you too." She dropped her arms and took a step back and looked around. "Why did you have us meet at a wedding dress shop?"

"Where's Campbell?"

"He couldn't make it," she said, "but I brought a replacement. Give me your gun."

"Why?"

"Because you're not going to like Flynn's replacement."

"I promise not to shoot him."

"On your honor. What's left of it anyway."

I sighed. "Thank you, for that."

"Promise me."

"I promise."

She stared at me, and when she was sure I wasn't bullshitting her, she nodded. Then she went to the door and opened it.

Brandon Kilmartin strode in. Hazel-eyed with a thick

head of brown curls, he was far too good looking for me to ever trust him. Plus, Quinn had once had a childhood crush on him. I had to hate him for that.

"You," I stated.

"Petrovich," he greeted with a roguish grin. "Why is it you always need me when Quinn goes missing?"

"Fuck you."

"Boys," Barrett said. She looked at Kilmartin. "You may be Flynn's cousin and Noah's favorite person, but I will still knee you in the balls if you piss me off."

Kilmartin grinned and threw his arm around her shoulders. "I love feisty women." His Irish lilt was too damn charming, but for Quinn—and Barrett's sake—I managed to make peace.

"Thank you for being here," I told him gruffly. "We're in a world of shit."

"Before you go on, can we please sit down? And maybe you can tell me why we're in the back room of a wedding dress shop," Barrett said.

"A friend is letting us use this place. Her family has issues with the Abruzzos."

"Feuds are fun, aren't they?" Kilmartin said good-naturedly.

"They make the world go 'round," I muttered. I walked to the door to lock it, and then I hit the lights. The room's lamps were on, lending a warm ambiance. Ambiance with a lot of lace.

Barrett took a chair and sat down. I could tell she'd been limping a bit, which meant her hip was bothering her. She'd never complain, though.

Kilmartin took the chair next to her. I paced, unable to sit still. "Ori Abruzzo is actually Ori Abruzzo Marino."

Barrett blinked. "You've got to be fucking kidding me. I thought we killed all the Marinos?"

"He wasn't there that night we took out his brother," Kilmartin said.

Kilmartin had been with me the night we'd found Quinn drugged on a boat. The Italians had wanted me because I'd killed their leader and taken over their territory. I'd gotten hurt in the explosion, and Michael O'Malley had wanted retribution, so he'd gone after the Marinos. It was one big mafia clusterfuck. Fathers, brothers, bastard brothers all came out of the woodwork. To sum it up, the many-year feud was between the Italians and the Russians. The Scots had gotten involved and so had the Irish.

"Did Dimitri finally find something?" she asked. "Is that how you realized his last name was Marino?"

I shook my head. "I haven't heard from Dimitri. The wedding dress shop owner filled in that last piece for me."

"No doubt he'd hired a vigilante hacker to wipe his legal name from the web. I bet that's why you didn't figure out who he was," Kilmartin said.

"Don't poke the Russian bear," Barrett said. "We've got bigger issues than to see whose dick is bigger."

"Mine," Kilmartin and I said at the same time.

Barrett snorted. "My dick is the biggest."

"You don't have a dick," Kilmartin said with an eye roll. "If you did, I don't think you and Flynn would be together."

"By proxy, I have claim to Flynn's dick. Thus, my dick is the biggest." She made a move to demonstrate the size, but I put my hands on hers to stop her.

"Not now. Please, not now."

She grinned.

I sighed and finally took a seat in the third chair that was unoccupied. "I haven't even told you the worst of it. Growing up, Ori Marino was Igor Dolinsky's best friend."

Barrett's face paled. "No."

"*Da*. Ori's mother basically became Igor's."

"And you missed all this?" Barrett yelled.

"Ori is a common Italian name," I said, my voice tight with anger. Anger at missing this link. "And I had no idea his middle name was Abruzzo. Bastard was hiding in plain sight. None of us realized who he was." I looked at her. "How come *you* didn't research the name Ori Abruzzo the moment Quinn told you? What does that say about you?"

Barrett's face went cold with rage. "She didn't tell me his name."

"So do not point fingers at me," I said, my tone finally softening.

She inhaled a shaky breath and then nodded, letting it go. "You don't think…" She swallowed, not able to go on.

"Think what?" Kilmartin pressed.

"Think Ori is out to destroy me?" she finished.

I met Barrett's eyes. They were wide with terror. "He doesn't know," I told her. "He thinks I was the one who…"

Kilmartin frowned in confusion. "You guys are speaking in riddles. You know that, right?"

"Tell him," I told her.

"You sure?" she asked, voice soft.

I nodded. "I trust him. He's family. On both sides." I smiled at the irony. Brandon Kilmartin was related to Barrett by marriage, and he was a close family friend of Quinn's. I trusted Kilmartin.

Didn't mean I liked him, though.

"Sasha wasn't the one to actually kill Dolinsky," Barrett admitted. "I was the one who pulled the trigger."

Brandon's hazel eyes never wavered when he heard his cousin's wife admit that she'd murdered a man. "The story floating around was that you"—he looked at me—"were the one who betrayed him and put the bullet in his chest."

A lump of emotion settled in my throat. "Igor and I

had a deal many years ago. I was supposed to put him down if he ever got out of control. He knew it was possible. You couldn't be Olaf Dolinsky's son without worrying about it. I was his check and balance system. Barrett might have been the one to pull the trigger, but I was the one who'd set it up so that she could."

"Fuck," Kilmartin muttered.

"But if you didn't know after all these years," Barrett said. "Then it's possible that Ori doesn't know about me either."

"That's the thing, Barrett," I said. "Ori Marino has been lurking in the shadows for years, hiding his identity, working steps ahead of us. He might not know you were there or that you killed Igor. As far as going after Campbell… I don't know if he will. Marino might not even know what happened the night his father died."

"So for right now, he's only going after you?" she asked, her tone worried.

"And Quinn," Brandon voiced. "He's taken Quinn. Why? She had nothing to do with any of this."

"Because she belongs to me," I stated grimly. "And he knows I'll come for her."

Chapter 39
QUINN

I sat on the ledge of the window seat and stared out at the vineyard. It was beautiful—the vines were bathed in faint moon glow and every so often, the leaves would stir from the soft, cool breeze.

There was the sound of a key in the lock, and then the door opened. I didn't turn to see who it was. I didn't want to see an Abruzzo. Not even the one I was engaged to.

"Quinn," Ori said.

I pretended like I hadn't heard him. I brought my knees to my chest, trying to make myself as small as possible. Not that it mattered. Ori had already made me small.

When he'd caught me trying to leave, he'd taken me by the arm, stuck me in the car, and driven me to his grandfather's house. He hadn't used brute force—he hadn't had to—because I was terrified of him. Something had flashed in his eyes when he saw me trying to leave him, something dark and dangerous that must've been lurking near the surface. He'd been able to conceal it, all this time, and I'd been at a distinct disadvantage. I'd taken his words and believed them.

Why?

Because he was my fiancé?

Because I couldn't remember my past?

Because I hadn't wanted to?

"Quinn," Ori said, attempting to pull me from my thoughts. "I'm doing this for your own good."

Anger bloomed in my chest, but I still refused to give him the satisfaction of breaking down and speaking to him.

"There are people—enemies of mine—that want to hurt you."

"Your cousin is one of them," I spat, unable to hold it in any longer. I turned my head and burned him with my rage. "And now you're keeping me prisoner." I gestured to the room, the gorgeous comfortable room any guest would feel at home in. But I wasn't a guest, I was a prisoner. "Explain that to me, Ori, because I don't get it."

"You have to trust me." His dark eyes drilled into mine. "I see it on your face, Quinn. You think I'm out to hurt you. Have I hurt you?"

I swallowed but remained silent.

"Exactly. I won't ever hurt you. In fact, I'll do anything to protect you. Even if that means hurting my own family."

"Hurt your own family?" I repeated. "What did you do?"

"Are you sure you want to know?"

Did I?

I swallowed. "Did you find out why she did it?"

"Yes."

I waited for him to say more, but he remained silent. "But you won't tell me?"

"I brought you a present." He picked up the dinner tray on the bedside table which he'd carried into the room.

"You brought me food," I said. "That's not a present."

He set the tray down on the bay window seat and lifted the chafing dish. I expected the scent of Italian herbs, the aromas of food made with love and affection.

I did not expect the tangy scent of blood—or the delicate finger that rested in the center of a white china plate.

Vomit climbed up my throat, and I pressed a hand to my mouth.

"Look at me, Quinn." His tone was dark, commanding.

I slowly raised my eyes to his.

The hand not holding the lid to the chafing dish reached out to caress my jaw. "You are mine. I protect what's mine. Do you understand?"

I nodded even though I didn't. Even though the man in front of me was a monster in disguise. He'd lulled me into believing he was someone good, just because he loved me, just because he took care of me.

But he had put me in a room and locked me in.

He wasn't protecting me; he was making sure I couldn't leave him.

Swallowing, I looked away from the dainty finger.

"Sasha Petrovich is dangerous, Quinn."

My head whipped around to look at him.

"His name means something to you, doesn't it?" When I didn't answer, he grasped my chin and applied enough pressure to make me gasp.

"Let me make something very clear to you. Petrovich is a murderer and a liar, and when you get your memory back, you'll remember that he left you. You can't count on a man like that. You count on me. Do you understand?"

"Yes," I whispered.

He dropped my chin and set the chafing dish down, covering the offending sight.

"Is that why you hate him?" I asked. "Because I once dated him?"

Ori's dark eyes glittered with hatred. "I don't hate him for that. Your past with him means nothing to me."

I shrank away, wanting to close in on myself, wanting to leave this place, wanting to hide, wanting to remember. But remembering my life seemed like it would doom me further. Ignorance wasn't really bliss. Ignorance was an excuse not to face the grief and darkness I knew I was trying to block out.

"Three days," he stated. "Three days and we'll be married."

My heart dropped. I wasn't sure about anything except I didn't want to marry him. I didn't want to marry this man who I no longer recognized.

He lifted the tray from the ledge and walked to the door. With one last look at me, he smiled. "You'll be a beautiful bride."

Chapter 40
SASHA

"Are you sure this is a good idea?" Barrett asked from the driver's side of the car.

I leaned my head back against the seat and forced my eyes to remain open. "Didn't really have a choice, did I?"

Barrett gripped the steering wheel and kept her eyes on the road. "Guess not. But The White Company… You know how brutal they are."

"Well, they are mercenaries," I pointed out. "If there was any other way, don't you think I'd take it?"

We'd been driving for an hour. We'd left Kilmartin behind to watch Quinn—who at the moment—was staying at the Abruzzo vineyard. It wasn't enough for me. Quinn was out of my sight, and I was trusting someone else to keep an eye on her.

I wouldn't breathe deeply again until I had her in my grasp, until I got her away from Ori Marino who wanted to use her to destroy me.

"What if he's actually in love with her," I said, the thought coming from a deep, dark crevice of my mind.

"It might be better if he is. Then we don't have to worry about him hurting her."

"Igor hurt you," I pointed out. "When he broke your ring finger."

Barrett's mouth flattened.

"Sorry," I said.

"No, you're not. Besides, it's the truth. He didn't love me."

"Is that what you tell yourself?"

"Men out for revenge will burn everyone and everything to the ground. They don't care who they hurt or kill."

"Didn't mean Igor didn't love you. I knew him. And he did."

It was dark out, and we still had a few more hours to go.

After a few minutes of silence, I said, "I wish he'd just come after me. With a gun or a knife. But he didn't. He went after Quinn to get to me."

"You weren't even in the States. How the hell else was he going to come after you but go for the woman you loved?"

"Love," I corrected. "I love her."

"Funny way of showing it," she muttered.

"I'm in Italy, aren't I? On my way to see The White Company."

"You need their guns to storm the castle. Yeah, I get it. Create a diversion while you slip in and get Quinn."

"Not just that, but I'm taking on the Marinos, one of Italy's most powerful families."

"I assume you'll be handsomely rewarded by the other powerful mafia families in Italy for taking out their competition."

"A bi-product, nothing more. I will not do business with any Italian."

Barrett laughed. "And I said I'd only package cocaine for Mateo Sanchez for a year. Look how that turned out."

"You could've walked away from that deal after the year mark. Sanchez would've let you."

"Too damn lucrative," she pointed out.

"Sanchez would give you the moon if you asked him to. How many hearts do you have in your pocket, Barrett?"

"Doesn't matter. The only one I want is Flynn's."

"You're ruthless."

"Have to be," she said lightly. "In our world."

"Do you ever think about what would've happened if you'd... Never mind."

"If I'd what?"

"Stayed with Igor," I finished.

"I try never to think about that. That's the kind of thought that could keep me awake at night."

"Had *his* children. Become a Russian queen."

"Wouldn't have reigned for long, I don't think. You would've put him down eventually. Taken me down, too."

"No. I'd never take you down. Igor was...broken. In a way you never come back from."

"Aren't we all?"

"I guess."

"What about you? Are you still broken?"

"You tell me."

"You're the same," she admitted. "But not. And I'm not just talking about your face or your body. You're hard, closed off, even from me. It's like, you're here, and living and breathing, but you're not who you used to be."

"No. I'm not."

"Are you sure it's fair to Quinn? I mean, really fair to her. Coming back."

"Are you telling me I'm being selfish?"

"Aren't you?"

"What's with the answering the question with a question?"

"Why won't you answer?" She threw me a smile, but then it slipped. "It was difficult, returning to Flynn after being with Igor. I knew in my heart, I wanted to go back to him, rebuild, reestablish, and we made amends, I think. As best we could and eventually, we got there. But for a long time, when I'd sleep next to Flynn, we weren't alone."

"Are you saying you should've stayed with Igor?"

"No," she said adamantly. "But maybe I should've chosen myself. Maybe it would've hurt Flynn less in the long run. Anyway, I don't know what to say about you and Quinn. But she…she's strong in her own way. She's endured a lot. She's lost a lot. And maybe when this thing with Marino is over, and Quinn has her memories, the kindest thing you can do for her is to let her go. I mean really let her go. Don't give her false hope that you're going to return. Let her go, in peace, to mourn you."

I fell silent as I let Barrett's words pierce my heart. "Am I a bastard if I can't do that? Am I a bastard for wanting to stay and prove to her that I'm worth giving another shot? We were so happy. Once."

"It's not enough. Anyone can remember the good times. It colors your judgment."

"Well, Quinn doesn't have any memories right now. So it's up to me to remember the good and the bad for both of us. It's up to me to bring her back."

Barrett snorted with laughter. "You really believe that shit you're spouting, don't you?"

I grinned in wry humor and then sighed. "I don't know anything anymore except that I love her, and I want her. If that means I'm selfish, then that's the way it is."

"You can't let her go."
"I tried. It didn't stick."
"Be sure this time."
"I am, Barrett. I am."

Chapter 41
QUINN

A few hours later, a woman I didn't recognize brought me a plate of food. I wasn't hungry—not since Ori had shown me the "present" he'd given me.

I was in a den of hyenas. Ori's cousin had drugged me, trying to kill me. I still didn't know why.

Ori had brought me her finger on a platter.

Psychotic barbarian.

Had I missed this? Were there hints that I'd never picked up on? I pounded my head, wishing back my memory.

I paced the room. I was going out of my mind, stuck. I didn't even have the cell phone that Ori had gotten for me. Not that it mattered since I didn't know whom to call.

What was going to happen during the next three days? Was he going to keep me locked up here—Irish Rapunzel in a tower?

I had a flash of a memory. A woman with long dark hair, green eyes the same shade as mine, reaching out to stroke my cheek. She smiled, her entire face changing.

She'd been gorgeous before, but when she smiled, it was like she was illuminated from within.

"Which fairy tale do you want to hear before bedtime?" she asked.

"Tell me your favorite."

She smiled. "You say that every night. Are you sure you don't want to hear something else?"

I shook my head, my eyes already drifting shut. Ten-year-olds weren't too old for fairy tales, not when their mothers made sure to tell them that princesses didn't need princes to rescue them.

I smiled.

I remembered my mother. I remembered the night of her funeral. I remembered crying in Shannon's arms while we drank a bottle of sherry my parents had gotten at their wedding. I remembered Shannon's face and the fact that she was married and having a baby.

My childhood flooded me in a slide of images but came to a crashing halt when I thought of Sasha and Ori. How the hell were they connected?

The photograph on the wall of Nonno's house. The three boys had history. One was dead. One was my past. And the other…the other I was marrying in three days.

I was exhausted but wired. How the hell was I going to sleep in this house? This house of horrors where fiancés suddenly became wardens.

There was no love here. Only power.

I didn't know a lot, but I definitely knew I was some sort of bartering chip. A pawn on the chessboard with kings. But that was the thing about chess, right? Kings were the weakest pieces of all. They needed to be guarded. If the king fell, so did the empire.

The key in the lock startled me from my thoughts. I went to sit by the bay window and tried to appear composed and calm. How the hell was I supposed to face

Ori? I'd given him my body, my smiles, my love. It made me sick to think I'd all but begged him to give me a family.

Thankfully, it wasn't Ori who entered the bedroom but Nonno. Ori's grandfather strode in—he didn't shuffle like so many men his age—and closed the door. He looked at me from beneath bushy eyebrows.

"You eat?" he asked in English.

I raised my eyebrows, surprised that he deigned to speak to me in my native tongue, deigned to speak to me at all, actually.

"Well?" he demanded gruffly.

"No."

"No? Why not?"

"Kind of lost my appetite."

He sighed. "Ori brought you…"

"He brought me his cousin's finger."

"Not his cousin." He raised his own finger to point at me. "His cousin's widow. Camilla has always wanted Ori."

"And she thought killing me would clear a path to him?" Righteous anger bubbled in my belly. Hell hath no fury like a woman ignored. Or scorned.

"You are not the woman I would've chosen for him," Nonno said with a shrug. "But he's a man, and he chooses what he wants."

"Why did you come in here?" I demanded.

"I offered to do it for him."

"Do what?"

"Cut off her finger. But he's strong and knows what needs to be done."

I swallowed down bile that was threatening to rise up and spew all over the cream windowsill cushions.

Nonno smiled. "You're a beautiful girl. I don't know if you're smart." He paused. "Ori says you are. But how do I know? How do *you* know?"

I wanted to ask him where he was going with this. Then again, I didn't want him to pull out a knife and just start slashing.

"Do you think you're smart?" he inquired.

"Lately? Not so much."

Nonno chuckled, but then his face darkened, and I could see the man he used to be. The power he once held. Now, he was nothing more than a weak old man harassing a woman who was under lock and key.

"Why did you come in here?" I asked again, finally getting up from my seat. I wanted to face him as an adversary and not as a weakling.

"I don't know," he admitted. "I guess I wanted to see what you were made of." We stared at each other. "It is too soon to tell."

Chapter 42
SASHA

"My teeth have things growing on them," Barrett said.

I let out a tired laugh. "Do you tell your husband things like that?"

"Yes."

"Then I can't believe you still have an active sex life."

"I'm too fucking exhausted to laugh," Barrett said. "I need a shower and a toothbrush and a bed. Maybe a glass of scotch first."

"It's six in the morning."

"Still nighttime."

"Who have you become?" I asked in bemusement.

We were both shattered. Down was up, up was down. This was not how I wanted to meet The White Company. I was bound to do something stupid. Say something stupid. Beg. I needed them. I was going into the lion's den to steal a gazelle, and I needed hunters with big fucking weapons.

"How are we playing this?" she asked.

"Honestly? I have no fucking idea."

"I'll not talk. God," she muttered, "I wish I looked better."

I threw a smirk at her. "You don't look as bad as you think."

"You're just saying that."

"When have I ever lied to you?"

She thought for a moment. "Fair point. I still think we should stop off at a hotel and freshen up. Maybe catch a few hours of sleep."

"I don't think—"

"Actually, that's exactly what we're going to do." She cut the wheel and turned sharply.

I gripped the side of the door. "Hey, easy!"

"I've always wanted to do that," she said, throwing me a grin. Her eyes were lit with humor and adrenaline. How we hadn't crashed was beyond me. Then again, there were very few cars on the road at this hour. The sky was just starting to turn pink, but it wasn't yet daybreak.

"The White Company mansion is back the other direction," I said.

"We're both not thinking clearly. We need to sleep, we need to regroup, we need new clothes and more importantly…I have to remember how to be a woman."

"Explain that last line to me because I'm not following."

"Looks, Sasha. I use my looks. Remember?"

Oh, I remembered.

"Not just my looks," she went on. "It's more than that. I'm not going to be able to talk when we meet with them, but you'll still want to show me off. You'll still take me everywhere you go when you're in that mansion—and they won't know that I am more calculating than I am beautiful."

"Run away with me," I said with a straight face.

She laughed. "I'm going to ensnare them with my body

so they think I'm nothing more than a piece of ass—and that's when we surprise them."

"You sure this isn't just an excuse to spend my money in a hotel boutique?"

"I don't need your money," she reminded me. "I've got my own."

"Your husband's, you mean?"

She took her eyes off the road just long enough to look at me. "Who do you really think is dealing with the most powerful cartel in Argentina? It's not Flynn."

"Wait," I said, my mouth dropping open. "Are you saying your deal with Sanchez is *your deal with Sanchez*?"

Barrett smiled and turned her eyes back to the road. "Why do you think he sends me orchids every Christmas?"

"I thought that was just to piss off Campbell."

"Byproduct. *I* am in business with Mateo Sanchez. The SINS aren't."

"I do believe my mind has just been blown."

"You trust me, don't you?"

"More than anyone," I said fiercely.

She touched my arm quickly and then put her hand back on the wheel. "I don't know what they'll expect from us in exchange for their aid."

"Blood oaths. Just like they demanded blood from Duncan."

A few years ago, Campbell's surrogate brother Duncan went to The White Company. They'd extracted blood, gave him a few broken ribs, but then pledged their help. They'd followed through. Once they'd had payment, they stayed the course.

"They might require more than blood," she said softly.

I looked at her. "You're not—you're not thinking what I think you're thinking."

"I most definitely am."

"Then you're not coming in with me."

"Sasha—"

"I will not whore you out!"

"When have I ever whored myself out?" she demanded. "I didn't whore myself out when Flynn was in jail and Mateo wanted me as payment. I gave him something better than my body. Don't you see? We use that against them. The White Company are just men. Men who can be ruled by what's in their pants. They are mercenaries. They don't care about revenge or vendettas or bygones from years past. You give them payment, they give you their warriors. It's a transaction."

"Yeah, and I know what kind of transaction you're thinking of giving them."

"They beat the shit out of Duncan. What are you going to do? Take the same beating? Then who goes and gets Quinn? While they cause the diversion, who gets Quinn?"

"Kilmartin," I said automatically.

"You're going to let that man rescue your woman?" She snorted. "Way to go with that grand gesture. Furthermore, we don't know her mental state. We don't know if she remembers him or you or me."

I shook my head. "I'm too recognizable. Half my face is scarred. Marino is waiting for me to come for her. He expects it." I leaned back against the seat. Exhaustion cleared from my mind when I saw the full picture. "I *can't* get her, Barrett. He's all but holding her hostage. He will for sure kill her if I come for her."

"So what do we—no. No, you can't be serious."

"I am."

She shook her head. "I can't run quickly anymore. I can't scale walls or climb up a rope. I've never ever had to use brute strength to get out of a situation. I can't really start now."

"You have to, Barrett. You're the only one who could slip past during the mayhem. No one will expect a woman to rescue another woman."

"Oh my God," Barrett whispered. "You're going to make me do this."

"Yes."

"Fine," she snapped. "But I want a really good fucking costume. I want to dress like Zorro."

"Yeah," I said with a laugh. "Because that's how you remain undetected."

Chapter 43

SASHA

We found a modest hotel—there wasn't anything overly opulent on our route. Barrett didn't care about opulence. Sure, the both of us had grown accustomed to the lifestyle. We hadn't been born into it, and we'd had to learn that money opened doors. Even ones with difficult locks. She'd adapted quickly and now walked with the air of an entitled queen. Benevolent but entitled, nonetheless.

Quinn, on the other hand, had been born into wealth. There were struggles she'd never faced, and yet I'd never call her weak. She hadn't had to work for anything in her life, but that didn't seem to matter when we were together. She wasn't lazy, just taken care of. Doted on. Her father had given her everything, maybe to make up for the loss of her mother as a teenager. But Quinn was exceedingly generous, loyal, and brave. She'd loved me—and would've loved me even if I hadn't been the leader of the Russian mafia. I was wrapped up in the life. She hadn't tried to separate it and had loved all of me. Every dark piece and every part that didn't belong to her. Quinn might've looked different than me on the outside, but she loved the same. Demanding everything and settling for nothing less.

"Two rooms or one?" the hotel clerk asked in English. His eyes skated across both of us. We looked like hell. It would take more than a change of clothes and a shower to get us looking right.

"Two—with a connecting door." Barrett handed over a credit card and looked at me and winked. "Untraceable," she mouthed.

The attendant nodded, typed on the keyboard, and then handed us two sets of keys and gave the credit card back to her. "Anything else I can do for you?"

She placed it in her purse. "Yes. We'll need two full breakfasts sent up to our rooms. Also, I need someone to run to the boutique next door. I wear a size—you should be writing this down."

The attendant's mouth dropped open, but he closed it quickly. "*Signprina*—"

"*Signora,*" she corrected immediately and held up her ringed hand. "I realize this might not be something you normally do. Charge it to the card on file. Double if you need. He needs a new suit." She looked over at me. "Give him your measurements."

As we rode the elevator up to our floor, I started to laugh.

"What's funny?" she demanded.

The doors opened and we stepped out. "You weren't taking any shit from that guy."

She grinned and then let out a full-on belly laugh. "Yeah, I didn't, did I? Usually I'm much more…"

"Smiley, flirty, nice."

"Thanks for those word choices." She shook her head as we walked down the carpeted hallway. "I didn't have the time, energy, or inclination to be nice. So I threw a credit card down and called it a day. Sometimes it's just easier, ya know?"

She must've been plugged into my brain since she was saying everything I'd already been thinking. We arrived at our doors, two right next to each other. The moment I got inside my room, I stripped out of my jacket and kicked off my shoes.

There was a knock on the connecting door. I strode to it and opened it. Barrett came into my room and flopped down into a chair. "You shower first."

"We have two separate showers," I reminded her. "We can shower at the same time."

"Yes, but someone has to be here when they bring the food and the clothes."

"You really think they'll bring that up here in the twenty minutes it would take to shower?"

Her smile was devilish. "My guess would be six."

"Six what?"

"Six people are going to come up here all at once, with everything I asked for. Ah, crap. I forgot to ask for make-up." She got back up. "I'll call down real fast. And you definitely shower. You're smelling a little ripe."

I whipped off my sock, balled it up, and threw it at her. Laughing, she dodged it, and then disappeared into her own bedroom. A moment later, I heard her voice as she spoke to the front desk. She'd pitched her voice soft and low.

The normal Barrett. Or at least the Barrett the world knew.

I stripped off the rest of my clothes when I got into the bathroom and then turned on the faucet. I stepped under the hot water and moaned out loud. It was that good. I washed quickly, my hands refusing to linger on the puckered skin on the right side of my body. After countless surgeries and skin grafts, it still didn't look right. It would never look like it once had, but I no longer dwelled on it.

More importantly, I was no longer embarrassed about it.

I shut off the water and reached for the towel. Wrapping it around my waist, I stepped out of the shower. I leaned over and smeared away the steam on the fogged-up mirror. It was true I was no longer embarrassed about my burned body, but my appearance was now a bit jarring. I still thought of myself the way I'd always been. My reflection was a shocking reminder that I wasn't.

Barrett was sitting on my bed, digging into her breakfast, when I came out of the bathroom. Her eyes landed on my body and her fork stilled.

"Like what you see?" I taunted.

She set her fork down and got up from the bed. I could see the purplish shadows under her eyes, the exhaustion in the lines around her mouth. I steeled myself as she drew closer, as one would approach a feral animal. Her steps were slow, purposeful. She reached out and touched my right shoulder. Her hand was cool against my heated skin.

"Fuck me," she whispered and shook her head.

"Is that an offer?"

"Stop," she said without any anger. She was still looking at my body. "You don't need to put on a show for me."

I fell silent and let Barrett have her fill.

"I've never seen it," she said.

"I've shown you mine, now show me yours." The scar on her knee was visible when she wore a shorter skirt, but I had no idea what the scar on her hip looked like.

She raised an eyebrow. "Will that make you feel better?"

I shrugged and tossed her a smile. "I was just

wondering if I'd be able to see the color of your underwear."

"White granny panties," she said automatically.

"Yeah, right."

"For me to know and for Flynn to find out," she said, a not so subtle reminder that she was married. Married to a man I actually liked and respected. Still, you could love someone and still want to fuck other people. It wasn't a crime.

"Wipe that look off your face," she said with an expression that reminded me of a schoolteacher. "You wouldn't make a pass at me. Just like you wouldn't cheat on Quinn."

"Quinn and I aren't together. And fidelity doesn't really play a role when someone walks away and the other gets engaged to a Marino out for my blood."

Barrett's hand dropped from my shoulder. "They brought clothes." Grabbing her plate, she turned around to let me dress in semi-privacy.

"I doubt Quinn knew who Ori really was when she started dating him," Barrett said, picking up the thread of our earlier conversation. "I mean, look how hard it was for us to discover his real last name. She probably didn't even know she should've been watching her back."

"That makes me feel worse, not better, because it means I left her unprotected."

"How were you to know? Dimitri was looking out for her. Flynn and I tried to check in with her, but Quinn is Quinn."

"Headstrong, independent, gorgeous—like another woman I know."

Barrett snorted. "Can I turn around now? It's hard to have this conversation with a window."

"I'm decent." I pulled on sweats and then took a seat on the bed. "Why are you in my room?"

"I had them bring the food in here. So I stayed to eat."

Nodding, I reached for a piece of bacon on her plate. Barrett was Barrett, and she let me have it. She picked up an orange slice and devoured the fruit before discarding the rind.

"My turn to shower. Our meeting with The White Company is tonight at sundown. I was thinking we could sleep until then."

"Sounds good. Not like we can really prep for this kind of meeting."

"Exactly." She got up, took one of the glasses of grapefruit juice, and headed for her room.

"I haven't been with anyone," I admitted. "Since her."

My words made her halt, but she didn't turn around.

"I walked away. Doesn't mean I stopped loving her."

"Tell her that," Barrett suggested. "Not me. I've already forgiven you for leaving."

Chapter 44

SASHA

There was only so long a body could go on adrenaline before it crashed and burned into an inferno. Barrett had been right about checking into a hotel for a few hours. I managed to fall asleep and thankfully, I didn't even dream of Quinn.

When the alarm went off, I rolled over and slapped my hand over it. I flipped onto my back and looked toward the window. The dying afternoon light was only a faint glow between the drawn curtains.

"You awake?" Barrett called through the open door to our connected rooms.

"With you yelling? *Da.*"

She grumbled and cursed at me, and before I knew it, she flopped down on the bed next to me. "You sure you want to do this?"

"You keep asking me that."

"Just answer the question, smart ass. If you changed your mind about going to The White Company, I could call Flynn, get the boys here. It would be faster than getting your men all the way from the States."

"It's not a matter of backup," I explained, "but the matter of the *right* backup."

"It's going to be a bloodbath."

"On multiple accounts," I agreed. "But as long as we get her out of there…"

"As long as we get her out of there, you don't care what happens to you. That's what you were going to say, wasn't it?"

I looked up at the ceiling. "Would you die for Campbell?"

She sighed. "All right, Sasha. All right."

"You'll stop trying to talk me out of this?"

"Yeah."

"Your word, Barrett."

"You have my word. But I swear to God, Sasha Petrovich, if you die, I'll find a way to bring you back to life just so I can kill you myself."

We fell silent. The minutes ticked by. I knew we needed to get up and get ready. Eat. Prepare for battle.

"It would've been so much easier, you know," I said finally.

"What?"

I looked at her and grinned. "If you'd just fallen in love with me from the beginning."

She let out a laugh. "Ah, Sasha. You don't deserve a woman with a divided heart. And mine was pretty splintered."

"What about Quinn's heart? She's engaged to him."

"After a few weeks," she reminded me. "With a case of amnesia. He must've told her a golden tale of love and perfection. She's not herself right now."

"I can't fault her, can I? I did tell her to move on, love again."

"Would you do it differently? If you could go back, would you do it differently? Even as far back as Igor?"

"No." I paused. "I'd do it all the same."

"Really? You would? Knowing what its cost you?"

"I don't know, Barrett. I kind of believe it all unfolds how it's supposed to. Without Igor, there never would've been you, I never would've lost you, I never would've found Quinn. See? How can I have any regrets, even when I've made the wrong choices?"

"You didn't lose me," she said quietly.

"Right, because you were never mine to lose."

Her hand snaked out to lace her fingers through mine. "I didn't think it was possible to love two men at the same time. But I can. I do," she corrected. "Losing you would destroy me just as much as losing Flynn."

She brought our hands to her lips and pressed a gentle kiss there. "I know it's not the same for you. I know you love me, but if I died, you'd find a way to go on. If Quinn dies… I fear for the world."

"If she dies. I'll burn the fucking world to the ground."

"Ah, there he is." She looked at me and released my hand. "Pick up that tarnished crown, Sasha. The throne—it's always been yours."

"Fuck me. No wonder men go to war for you."

Barrett sat up and hugged her knees to her chest. "It's also why I need to be in the room when you speak to The White Company." She shook her head and laughed.

"What?"

"I'm just thinking… What would've happened if Helen of Troy had been more than a hot piece of ass? Troy got sacked because Paris couldn't keep it in his pants for a beautiful woman with no substance."

"Maybe the bards got it wrong."

She wrinkled her nose. "Maybe they got it right."

"You're no Helen of Troy. Neither is Quinn."

Barrett's eyes lit up. "Then let's go sack the hell out of Troy."

Barrett held on to my arm as we walked through the lobby. From anyone else's standpoint, we looked like a couple. Beauty and the Beast. Barrett held on to my arm because she was uncomfortable in heels. She didn't wear them often, not since the accident that shattered her hip and knee.

When I saw her putting them on, she'd smiled and assured me she could handle it. "Heels," she'd said, "are just another weapon in a woman's arsenal."

The boutique had brought her a white dress that hit a few inches above the knee. It cut into a V in front and back. She'd twirled up her auburn hair and stuck a pin through it. Classic pearls graced her ears and throat. I wore a gray three-piece suit with a white shirt and black tie. You dressed to impress when you met with The White Company.

Neither one of us really knew what to expect. Duncan hadn't shared his experience. Said he was sworn to secrecy. So whatever went on tonight, it was between me, Barrett, and The White Company.

"You didn't tell me how pretty I am," Barrett said as we waited for the hotel valet to bring the car around.

"You look pretty," I said dismissively.

"Nope. Try again."

"Barrett," I growled.

"You have to drive. I can't in heels."

"I'd planned on driving."

She sighed. "You're not going to let me distract you, are you?"

"Do you have a bottle of vodka in that very tiny purse?"

"It's called a clutch. And no, I don't."

The car drove up, and a hotel agent helped Barrett into the passenger side. I walked around to the driver's side and forced my head into the moment. I was going to meet The White Company with Barrett. It would've been easier without her. I would only worry about her. But if I'd learned anything about Barrett, it was that she could take care of herself.

"We got this," she said.

I pulled away from the curb. I wasn't worried about The White Company. I was worried about Quinn and leaving her in the hands of a man who would do anything to see me go down.

"I could always tell him I was the one who killed Igor," she said.

"Like hell you could."

"Do you think he'd shoot a pregnant woman?"

I nearly swerved. "You're pregnant? Are you fucking kidding me? Does Campbell know? He's gonna fucking kill me when he realizes you—"

"Relax. I'm not pregnant."

"Jesus Christ, give me a heart attack."

She laughed. "Like I said. Use whatever is in your arsenal."

Chapter 45
SASHA

"Brandon texted," Barrett said, stuffing her cellphone back into her white purse—clutch—whatever the hell it was.

"What did he say?"

"No change. She's still at the vineyard. No sign of Ori."

"No sign of Marino? Where the hell is he?"

"Don't know," Barrett said with a shrug. "But like you said, Ori would know if you came for her, so he's probably on the lookout for anyone that doesn't…fit in?"

"You mean Kilmartin is keeping a lookout from a distance."

"A tree, actually."

"Jesus."

"And what's with that?"

"With what?"

"The last name thing. Do you realize you call Brandon *Kilmartin* and Flynn *Campbell?*"

"I call Duncan and Ramsey by their last name, too."

"The only one you don't call by his last name is Dimitri. Why is that?"

"Dimitri is Russian."

"Yes, I know. That's not an explanation, by the way. Just a fact."

I sighed. "Dimitri is one of my own. It's different."

"Hmm. You call me by my first name."

"I do."

"You call Quinn by her first name."

"Where are you going with this?"

"Is this because we're women?"

I raised an eyebrow and looked at her. "Are you sure you're not pregnant? You're acting fucking weird."

"No, I'm not pregnant," she snapped. "I just want to know why you're determined to keep your distance after all these years."

"It's easier. And habit. It's not even a conscious choice."

"You don't call my sons by their last names."

"That would mean I'd call four Campbell men *Campbell*. It would be confusing and I—holy shit."

"What?"

"You did it."

"Did *what*?"

"Distracted me."

She turned her head and grinned. "Damn right."

My laughter echoed in the car, a full-on belly laugh. It suddenly felt like everything was manageable. There were criminals and then there were mercenaries, but I could do this.

"Glad I'm here?" she fished.

"Damned glad," I admitted.

A half an hour later, it was completely dark, and I turned the car off the main road onto a paved brick one. We arrived at a large iron gate, medieval in style.

"I forgot to ask Duncan if he saw heads on pikes when he was here," Barrett said, peering up at the iron posts.

"I think it's better if we don't know."

"Point. There's no security guard to check our IDs or wave us through. That's how you know these guys are so dangerous they don't need normal security measures."

The iron gate drew open, and I drove the car forward.

"Got your armor in place?"

She sent me a sideways smile. "How's my lipstick? Bright? Whorish?"

"You really want me to answer that question?" I said with a surprised laugh. Only Barrett could lighten the mood when we were about to get our heads blown off.

"I want them thinking about my mouth," she said.

"Mission accomplished." We drove up the windy road until we came to the mansion. It was bold, white, austere in the moonlight with arches and towers.

I looked at Barrett. "Is this a home or a church?"

"You got me." Barrett's gaze was full of awe. "I live in a restored Scottish castle and right now, I'm kind of jealous of these guys."

The heavy, ornate wooden doors opened, and two men dressed in dark suits strode out. Mankind had no natural predator. We were at the top of the food chain, the destroyers of the earth. Yet these men were no ordinary men. These were men who were the shadows, embraced the darkness, and killed for hire. They didn't take money as payment and just because someone would pay their price, didn't mean The White Company would accept it. They called the shots, negotiated the terms, and decided who they'd fight for.

Barrett's side door opened, and she reached her hand out for help. For a moment it looked like no one would help her, but she waited patiently. Finally, the man caved and offered his hand.

My door opened and I slid out. Nodding at the man who held my door open, I buttoned my suit jacket. Barrett waited for me at the bottom of the white marble steps, and when I came to her side, we slowly ascended the stairs together.

Though the doors to the mansion were open, there was no light coming from inside; it was just a black hole waiting to swallow us both.

Barrett looked at me, and her lips pulled into an amused smile. Only her eyes revealed her true trepidation —and I was the only one who would notice because I'd known her for years. But in true Barrett fashion, she tossed her head back, squared her shoulders and said, "Into the dragon's mouth we go."

Chapter 46
SASHA

Dark soon gave way to light as candles along the pathway flared to life. There were attendants in the shadows, all in dark clothing, moving seamlessly.

The heavy doors shut and Barrett's hand in mine tightened. We continued to walk. We walked until the marble floor of the foyer spilled into a large room that was on par with receiving rooms of ancient kings. There was opulent show of wealth and then there was simply having it.

The White Company's wealth rivaled the Vatican's. Priceless art and furniture decorated the room. The floors glimmered with inlaid gold and silver. A single chair—a throne—rested on a raised wooden platform.

Tapestries hung from the walls, and marble statues stood in corners. Museum curators would give their own two eyes for a shot at showcasing even just a few of these pieces. This room was meant to overwhelm, it was meant to ensnare, it was meant to remind every outsider who entered that we were nothing more than peasants begging for a king's hand out.

It was nearly impossible not to gawk, but Barrett and I

managed not to. Instead, she moved closer to my body and whispered in my ear, "You know they're watching our reaction from some video camera."

I turned my head, so my mouth was flush against her ear. "Of course they are."

She threw back her head and laughed. Her eyes sparkled with intent. She wanted to put on a show. Gripping my lapels, she leaned close and whispered, "Trust me."

Before I could reply, Barrett slipped from my grasp and sauntered toward the ornate throne. I forced my jaw not to drop when Barrett gently lowered herself onto the chair. Her arms rested on the decorative armrests, and she frowned.

"Huh," she said. "I thought this throne would've been more comfortable." She kicked off her heels and then draped herself across it. "Nope. That doesn't work either. Who would want to sit here?"

"Catherine de Medici," came a voice. A shadowy figure stepped out from between two drapes. Though I couldn't tell his age, I could tell his size. Big. Bigger than me, bigger than Campbell. Bold and wide, but something told me he used his size to intimidate, but actual skill to inflict any sort of pain.

"The wife of King Henry the II of France," Barrett said. "Queen Mother, regent, and a ruthless woman." Her red smile widened. "I admire her."

The man's mouth parted into a smile of his own. He walked toward the throne, keeping his eyes on Barrett. When he stopped a few inches from the throne, he gave a slight bow.

Barrett laughed. "Please, don't stand on ceremony." She held out her hand. "Barrett Campbell."

The man took it and brought it to his lips. "Barrett

Campbell. Campbell," he repeated. "Why do I know that name?"

With her hand still in his grasp, she managed to swing her legs around and stood. "I'm married to Flynn Campbell."

"Of course you are," he said, amusement lurking at the corners of his mouth. "And you've come to see me because…"

She cocked her head to one side. "I have a feeling you know a lot more than you're letting on—and if that's the case, you know it's not me who came for your help. May I introduce you to Sasha Petrovich?"

The man's eyes slid from Barrett's face, but he still hadn't dropped her hand. "Sasha Petrovich." His gaze raked over me. "Hmm."

We stared at one another for a moment, and then he nodded. "I'm intrigued. Come, we will have dinner, and we will discuss."

"I never have dinner on a first date," Barrett stated, taking the offered arm.

He laughed. "Your husband must enjoy your quick tongue."

"On so many occasions," she purred.

I trekked behind them, not wishing to interrupt. Barrett was putting on a show. She'd play the forward one, and I'd play…well, I hadn't decided what I was supposed to play. The man still hadn't introduced himself.

We walked through the curtains into a dining room with a long table that could easily sit thirty. At the moment, only three seats were set with white china rimmed with gold. Silver candelabra rested in the center of the table. Drippy white tapered candles turned everything into gilded masterpieces. It brought out the cinnamon strands in Barrett's auburn hair.

The man watched her take it all in. I watched him watch her. His eyes hid his interest, but I could read a man in lust. He turned his body ever so slightly toward her and leaned over almost like he wanted to sniff her hair.

Thankfully he didn't try it. Barrett was here, under my protection, and I would've hated to resort to violence to prove it. It would only make my blood payment that much more expensive.

"You haven't introduced yourself," Barrett pointed out.

"Angelo Moretti." He pulled out Barrett's chair and she sat. Angelo pushed the chair forward and then reached over Barrett to pick up the napkin and place it in her lap.

I had to stop my eye roll.

Angelo looked at me and gestured to the chair across from Barrett. "Please."

No one helped me with my chair. I sat down and leaned back, projecting lazy insolence. Angelo took his seat, and immediately the soup course was served.

Once the servants cleared out, Angelo picked up his spoon and dipped it into his bowl. "Mushroom soup. Enjoy."

Barrett reached for her silverware, but I remained steadfast. Angelo noticed.

"You don't like mushroom soup?"

"Love it," I stated.

He raised a dark eyebrow. In the dim lighting, it was still difficult to distinguish his age. I had him pegged in his forties. He was fit and muscular, but there were the tiniest lines at the corners of his dark eyes.

"I like to discuss business during dessert," Angelo said. "And until then, you are my guests. So please, entertain me." With that last statement, he swiveled his head and gave all his attention to Barrett.

"Should I sing for your entertainment?" she asked.

His lips spilled into a smile. "Can you sing?"

"No."

Angelo chuckled. "What can you do?"

"A little of this, a little of that."

Watching Barrett flirt was making me lose whatever appetite I'd had. I watched in dumb amazement as Barrett carried on witty banter while simultaneously clearing her soup bowl and then the duck course.

Neither one of us reached for our wine. Neither did Angelo, I noticed. We were all playing our roles. I just hadn't figured out Angelo's. As dinner wore on, the hour grew later, which meant another hour Quinn was in Marino's hands. But pushing Angelo into discussing business before he was ready was a sure-fire way not to get his help.

When the biscotti and anisette were served, Angelo leaned back in his chair and said, "She was a charming guest. You. You sit there, hardly eat a bite, sulking."

"The food was delicious," I said genuinely.

Angelo waved his hand. "Ah, but you have things on your mind. Things you wish to discuss. I am ready to discuss."

Now he sounded like a crime lord.

"You're familiar with the Abruzzo family, I imagine," I said.

Angelo reached for the plate of biscotti and broke off the end. Turning to Barrett, he offered it to her with a smile. With a smile of her own, she took it and popped it into her mouth. Satisfied that she was enjoying the cookie, Angelo turned his attention back to me.

"I'm familiar with them, yes."

"They have something of mine."

"Do they?" Angelo murmured. "Artifact or antique?"

"My woman," I growled.

Angelo sighed. "All the legendary wars start because of a woman."

"Truth," Barrett stated and then sipped her anisette. She was watching me over the rim of her glass, silently warning me to be careful.

"What is it you want from me?" Angelo wondered. "We aren't the Italian version of the American SWATS. We don't do rescue missions. We are warriors for hire. Nothing more."

"I need a diversion," I said. "I'll handle the extraction."

Angelo played with the stem of his snifter glass. "This will cost a lot."

I ground my jaw. "Name your price."

Angelo's gaze slid from me to land on Barrett. "Her."

Barrett snorted but kept silent. She even reached for another biscotti.

"She's not mine to give," I said. "Name something else."

"I don't want anything else. This is my price. A night with her."

"*Her* has a name," Barrett said mildly.

Angelo smiled.

"I'm married," she said.

"I don't care. Payment is payment."

Barrett pushed her snifter aside and reached for his. Angelo smiled and let her have it. "There has to be some rules."

"Barrett," I warned.

She waved her hand at me. "We need Quinn back. Flynn will understand."

Like hell Campbell would understand. He'd murder me if I let this happen. But Barrett shot me a warning look that told me to back off. I didn't really have a choice. Angelo didn't want payment from me.

"I thought all payment had to be made in blood," I blurted out, a last-ditch effort to free Barrett.

"Normally, that's the case, yes," Angelo said. "But I can demand any payment I want."

"Eyes on me, Angelo," Barrett said.

Angelo's eyes snapped to hers, and his mouth parted slightly. He was excited, ravenous.

Barrett smiled. Angelo saw a woman enjoying herself.

I saw a black widow.

"You want a night with me, yes?" she went on.

"Yes," Angelo agreed.

"I'll give it to you," she said. "Willingly. If you beat me in one-on-one combat."

Angelo threw his head back and laughed. "Is this your version of foreplay?"

Barrett smiled slightly. "Do we have a deal? I'll spend the night with you if you beat me one-on-one. Then Sasha gets The White Company's help."

"And if I lose?" Angelo taunted. "Which I won't."

She cocked her head. "If you lose, the payment is forfeit and Sasha still gets your help." She held out her hand. "Deal?"

Chapter 47

SASHA

"You weren't supposed to talk. What happened to that plan?" I asked Barrett.

"I lied."

"You're fucking certifiable."

Barrett grinned. "You have no faith in me."

"Faith? You're nearly half his size. You have no combat training. And you favor your right side."

"Shut up," she growled. "Or he'll hear you."

I looked at the other side of the training room. Angelo was dressed in a pair of athletic shorts and no shirt. His muscles strained, his bones popped as he stretched. "He's going to figure it out," I told her. "From watching you walk."

"So let him," she said. "Do I look ready?"

Barrett was wearing a pair of spandex shorts and a black sports bra. She'd given me her pearls, which were currently tucked away in my suit jacket breast pocket. Her hair was still in a fancy uptwirl with her hairpin stuck through it. It was better not to have it in a ponytail. He wouldn't be able to grab it that way.

There were only the three of us in the training room, so at least there wouldn't be an audience. But I didn't think for a second that Barrett would actually win. Not with the odds against her and her physical limitations. Not to mention she wasn't trained. I stood a chance against Angelo because of what I'd done this last year. But I had no idea the man's skill.

"If you have to spend the night with Angelo, I'd better just cut off my own balls and send them to your husband. It would save him the trouble."

Barrett flashed a smile. "No one's balls will exchange hands. Trust me."

"Barrett!" Angelo called, striding closer. "Are you ready?"

"Absolutely."

The two of them took to the center of the mat. There was no referee, no one to gauge the fight, no one except me.

I sent up a silent prayer that Barrett had some sort of badass magical fighting powers that would get us out of this, and she'd walk away with me tonight and not spend it in Angelo's bed.

"Ready. Go!" I called.

They circled each other. Angelo lunged, but Barrett evaded his grasp. She even managed to land a punch to his stomach. Angelo laughed as if it was nothing more than a minor distraction.

"Ow!" Barrett shook out her hand. "Damn, it's like hitting a brick wall."

Angelo grinned, arrogance ricocheting off him. "You could give in now. Gracefully. Petrovich will get the backing of The White Company."

"Oh, I'm not ready to give in," Barrett taunted. "It means more when you make a man really earn it."

Angelo launched himself at her. She twisted her body, bent nearly in half, and dodged Angelo in one smooth movement. Barrett laughed. "You could give in!"

The huge man growled, kicked out his foot and caught the back of her bad knee. Barrett went down on the mat and Angelo pressed his body on top of hers, straddling her. His thighs nearly touched her chin.

"Looks like I win," he said, his voice pitched low.

I swallowed. All my hope sinking that Barrett hadn't been foolhardy. I should've known it was forced bravado.

"No," I called out. "Get up. I don't need your help. Barrett—"

"Shut up, Sasha," she wheezed. "This is between me… and Angelo."

"Do you concede?" Angelo asked, staring down at Barrett with naked lust—and something like admiration. How many women had offered to fight him? How many men, for that matter?

"Do I concede?" Barrett asked. Her right hand went for the hairpin. Before Angelo could dip his head and take what was rightfully his, Barrett plunged the hairpin into Angelo's thigh.

He roared in pain and reared back, giving Barrett ample opportunity to scramble out from under him. She pulled the pin from his thigh. Gripping it in her hand, she shot me a look.

I shook my head. "I should've known about the hairpin. It *is* your signature weapon."

Barrett grinned and then turned her attention back to Angelo who had a hand to his thigh and was staunching the flow of blood. "Blood payment complete. The White Company will help Sasha."

He nodded slowly, his dark eyes surveying her. Angelo

licked his lips. "You wouldn't want to stay and bandage me up, would you?"

"No." She patted his cheek. "I think that would give you the wrong idea." She looked at me. "Ready?"

I nodded. We walked out of the training room and down the hallway. A man waiting at the door handed Barrett her heels, dress, and coat. It wasn't until we were in the car driving back to our hotel that I said, "You're not worried?"

"About?" Barrett wiped the hairpin on the white dress, effectively ruining it.

"About Angelo trying to make you a widow."

She laughed. "No. I'm not worried."

"You think he'll keep his word and send The White Company when I need them?"

"Yes. Otherwise, I know a certain hacker who would have no trouble blowing the lid off their operation."

Gripping the steering wheel, I finally let out a full-on laugh. We zoomed through the night, heading back to our hotel to celebrate and plan for how we were going to get Quinn.

"What have you been doing while I've been gone?" I asked.

"While you were training to be a ninja, I was learning Krav Maga."

I laughed again. "God damn. Seriously?"

"Seriously." She shot me an amused grin. "I went down on purpose. I knew he was going to go for my knee."

"You went down on purpose? Why?"

"I was getting bored. I wanted to end it. So," she shrugged, "I let him think he won."

"You know we're not allowed to tell Campbell. What happens with The White Company has to remain—"

"It'll be our little secret," she promised. "Better that way, actually. I did promise him I wouldn't use my feminine wiles on any other man except him."

"On behalf of the rest of mankind, I think that's probably a good idea. We'd never stand a chance."

Chapter 48

QUINN

I stared at myself in the mirror. A shadow of a woman stared back. My lashes were coated with mascara, blush tinted the skin of my overly pale cheeks, my mouth was stained red.

The lace veil flowed down my back and trailed past my dress. The wedding dress made of Italian lace. The dress I'd wear to become Ori's wife.

I swallowed a bout of tears, glad most of my memories hadn't returned. I no longer wished to know what I was missing because the future I didn't want loomed before me.

It had been three days since Ori had dictated that I'd marry him, and I hadn't seen him since. And now, my wedding day had arrived. There were no tears of joy, no best friends or mothers to blot my lashes to make sure I didn't smear my makeup. Today, my heart was not full, but empty.

There was a quick rap on the door and then it opened. Nonno strode in wearing an impeccable three-piece black suit. "It is time," he announced.

I swallowed and went to him. He guided me down the stairs and through the house, out toward the vineyard where the ceremony was being held. When we'd come to Italy, I thought I would be married in the small church, but apparently, even that sham of a beautiful picture had burned into a pile of ashes.

The day was bright and cool. White chairs had been set out and all the guests—all fifty of them—rose. A string quartet played the Wedding March, and on Nonno's arm, I trudged toward the man who would not only become my husband, but my captor.

Ori's dark gaze tracked my every step. He looked solemn, stoic in his black suit. Not at all how I pictured my future husband on our wedding day. I didn't expect tears, either, but maybe a smile? A glimmer of amusement. But Ori gave me nothing.

Nonno stopped, kissed my cheek, and then gave my hand to Ori who took it in his large one. He didn't squeeze my fingers to give me any sign of assurance. Instead, he turned us both toward the priest who started reciting the ceremony in Latin.

We both took Communion and then waited for the family to do the same.

Ori recited his vows—first in Italian and then in English.

I looked away from his gaze, peering out across the land, praying, wishing for someone to ride up on a horse and whisk me away. But there was no sign of any man from my past. No sign of *him*.

Ori's fingers tightened on mine, drawing my attention back to the moment, back to the moment when words would shackle me to this man for the rest of my life.

"Quinn," Ori growled, urging me to say the words.

"I do," I whispered. My voice was raspy, my throat parched.

Ori slid a delicate band onto my finger.

My name is Quinn O'Malley.

I am the wife of a monster.

I remember everything.

Additional Works

The Tarnished Angels Motorcycle Club Series:

Wreck & Ruin (Book 1)
Crash & Carnage (Book 2)
Madness & Mayhem (Book 3)
Thrust & Throttle (Book 4)
Venom & Vengeance (Book 5)
Fire & Frenzy (Book 6)
Leather & Lies (Book 7)
Heartbeats & Highways (Book 8 - preorder)

SINS Series:

Sins of a King (Book 1)
Birth of a Queen (Book 2)
Rise of a Dynasty (Book 3)
Dawn of an Empire (Book 4)
Ember (Book 5)
Burn (Book 6)

Ashes (Book 7)
Fall of a Kingdom (Book 8)

Others:

Peasants and Kings

About the Author

Wall Street Journal & USA Today bestselling author Emma Slate writes romance with heart and heat.

Called "the dialogue queen" by her college playwriting professor, Emma writes love stories that range from romance-for-your-pants to action-flicks-for-chicks.

When she isn't writing, she's usually curled up under a heating blanket with a steamy romance novel and her two beagles—unless her outdoorsy husband can convince her to go on a hike.